# HERE GHOST NOTHING

THE GHOST DETECTIVE SERIES #5

JANE HINCHEY

FREE BOOK OFFER

Want to get an email alert when the next Ghost Detective Mystery is available?

Sign up for my Reader's Group today,

https://janehinchey.com/starter-library/

and as a bonus, receive a FREE e-book of **Cupcakes & Curses!**

**Who dares wins!**

How can any self-respecting, slightly clumsy, highly caffeinated private eye pass up a dare? Short answer, she can't. Now I'm up a certain creek without a paddle trying to figure out how to live without coffee for an entire week!

With my mood sour, my temper frazzled, and my patience long gone, how am I meant to deal with this? And by this, I mean the dead body on my front lawn.

Before I can say *double espresso,* I've got a ghost whose transition to the afterlife is far from smooth, an overweight cat who is annoyingly vocal about his new (*definitely called for*) diet, and a mystery to solve that involves multiple visits to the local brewery… maybe there's a silver lining in all this craziness after all.

# 1

I'd been having the best dream. One where I owned a café and had unlimited access to coffee. We're talking affogato, Americano, caffe latte, caffe mocha, café au lait, cappuccino, espresso, espresso macchiato, latte macchiato, and everything in between. Coffee porn, if you like. And I did like it. Very much.

It was the third dream I'd had of its kind this week, all because of a stupid dare with my sister-in-law, Amanda. Why, oh, why did I let her bait me? Why didn't I just walk away? I knew this was her latest attempt to *fix me*. According to Amanda, my inherent clumsiness could be cured, and her latest remedy was to remove caffeine from my life. It had started involuntarily when she'd switched out my coffee pods for decaf behind my back.

Things had escalated from there. I couldn't let that transgression go unpunished. I'd switched her organic, herbal shampoo and conditioner for the cheapest supermarket brand I could find in retaliation. She'd been furious, and I'd been up in her face about messing with *my coffee,* which is when she issued the dare. One week without coffee.

*Easy!* I'd scoffed, shaking her hand to seal the deal. If I won, she vowed never to interfere in my life ever again. If I lost? I had to give up caffeine for good.

But something was pulling me out of the best dream in the world, something intruding and prodding me awake. I curled into a ball, tugging the comforter up around my chin, chasing the dream that was rapidly slipping from my reach with a desperation not to leave my blissful coffee hazed nirvana.

Then the music started. Softly at first but rising in volume. Something about a baby on fire. *Wha?* After a moment, I realized it was the dulcet tones of Pitbull singing Fireball, the ringtone I'd chosen for my new phone. Groaning, I pried open my eyes and felt around on the nightstand for it, succeeding in knocking it to the floor where Pitbull continued his woohooing.

I turned my attention to the dead guy standing at the foot of my bed.

"Can you get that?" My voice came out like rusty nails. No surprise since I'd taken to replacing coffee with whisky. I'd drag my body through a week of zero coffee and marinated in alcohol if it killed me.

"Um, the phone?" he asked, puzzled.

"Mmm." I lowered my lids.

Dead Guy cleared his throat. "I'm not sure—"

"Never mind." I reached an arm over the side of the bed, searching for the offending phone, reaching farther and farther until the inevitable happened. I tumbled out of bed to land with a thud on the floor.

"Are you okay?" Dead Guy looked concerned.

Ignoring him, I snatched up my phone. "What?"

"Just checking in." Amanda's voice was as welcome as a hoohaa waxing on a full moon.

"You're checking in at four-thirty in the morning?" I laid on the floor and stared up at the ceiling, admiring a particularly creative cobweb dangling from the light fixture.

"It's six, and you know it. I call the same time every day."

*Yeah, you do.* "To make sure I'm not dead," I grumbled. I hit a button on the phone to hang up, but it's entirely possible I'd called the pizza delivery place... it wouldn't be the first time. Heaving a sigh, I rolled to my side and dragged myself to my hands and knees then, using the side of the bed for leverage, to my feet.

I padded toward the bathroom, pointing a finger in the general vicinity of the dead guy. "Wait here." The trouble with ghosts was they had no sense of boundaries. Just because you could walk through walls doesn't mean you should. Especially when I was in the bathroom.

I sat on the toilet and listened to the scratching coming from the other side of the door. Rolling my eyes, I yelled, "Thor. Bandit. Quit it." Honestly, once they knew I was awake, the pair of them hounded me until I'd filled their kibble bowls. Only Thor, my big—emphasis on *big*—gray teddy bear of a cat, was on a diet. Which meant Bandit, my recently acquired raccoon, was also on rations. Not that Bandit seemed to mind. But Thor? The downside of having a talking cat was that you got to listen to their complaining. A lot.

After washing my hands and splashing water on my face, I flung open the door. The two furry critters greeted me with overexaggerated enthusiasm before bounding ahead, leading the way downstairs amidst compliments on how fresh and beautiful I looked this morning. All lies in hopes of getting more kibble out of me.

Dead Guy followed my entourage and now stood in my open plan living room. I cocked my head and studied him. He wore jeans, a nondescript T-shirt, loafers without socks, and a dusting of a five o'clock shadow on his square jaw. He looked vaguely familiar.

"Now?" he asked hopefully.

My shoulders slumped. I really needed caffeine for this. "Fine. Go ahead." I waved at him to continue.

"I think I'm dead," he said. *Oh God, I was woken from my slumber for this?* I did my best not to roll my eyes or call him Captain Obvious, for while he was new at being a ghost, I was all too familiar with them. My best friend Ben was a ghost, and I'd been seeing and talking with him for almost a year. I glanced around for any sign of Ben, but he'd yet to return from his nocturnal wanderings. Since he didn't need sleep, Ben amused himself by visiting insomniacs and watching Netflix or, preferably, the shopping channel with his blissfully unaware companions.

"I'm afraid so." Turning, I grabbed a glass and shoved it under the faucet. Opening the top drawer, I rummaged for pain killers, but the junk drawer failed to deliver, and I slammed the glass down a little harder than intended, the contents sloshing over the rim.

Dead Guy looked startled, and I forced myself to drag in a calming breath. It wasn't his fault I was hungover. Or caffeine-free. Why he was standing in my living room, though, was something I was curious about.

"Why are you here?"

"I was coming to see you." He looked toward the front of the house then back at me.

"Do you ghosts get a handbook or something? How did you even know I can see and talk to ghosts?"

He blinked. "I didn't. I was coming to see you when I…"

The penny dropped. "Oh! You mean, you were literally coming here to see me when you died?"

"Yes."

I pointed toward the front door. "You're here? On the other side of that door?"

"Yes."

Just to be sure, I took a step toward said door, pointing. "This door?"

"Yes."

"Why?"

He opened his mouth, hesitated, then snapped it closed, a frown pulling his brow low. "It's the darndest thing. I can't remember. I *know* I was coming to see you. I just don't know why."

"Right." It wasn't the first time this had happened. Death amnesia. It had happened to Ben, only he hadn't known he was dead, not to begin with. But once we'd worked it out, it had been left to me to solve the mystery of his murder because his memory of the event was buried so deep in his subconscious he couldn't access it. Not entirely surprising if you'd died a violent death.

"Since I don't know you, I'm assuming you were coming here to hire me." It wasn't an odd assumption since I ran Delaney Investigations, the private investigator business I'd inherited from Ben.

"Maybe, yeah. But I guess that doesn't matter anymore."

Right. Because he was dead, and according to him, he'd died at my front door. No wonder he'd found me. His ghost hadn't had far to travel. With a sigh, I trudged down the hallway to the front of the house and flung open the door. I was unprepared for the glare of sunlight and raised my arm to shield my eyes. No dead body on my doorstep. Stepping outside, I didn't have to go far before I found the dead guy face down on my lawn. The cause of death was apparent thanks to the great hulking knife sticking out of his back.

Reaching for my phone, I realized I was standing on my lawn in what I'd slept in, which was a tank and panties, and my phone was upstairs in my bedroom where I'd left it. Swiveling on my heel, I hurried back inside, thankful the house next door was vacant. No prying eyes of neighbors to catch me in my underwear. I snorted. Like they would worry about that over a dead body on my front lawn.

"If I were caffeinated, this wouldn't have happened," I said to myself, taking the stairs two at a time. Dead Guy followed.

"Me getting killed?"

"What? No. That was inevitable. No, I mean I wouldn't have gone outside in my underwear, nor would I have left my phone upstairs. Rookie mistakes. I'm usually more alert than this."

"Right. So, have a coffee then."

"If only I could." I sighed. It sounded suspiciously like a moan. Scooping up my bra from the floor, I rummaged in a drawer for a clean T-shirt and pair of jeans and disappeared into the bathroom to finish dressing.

"Tell me what you remember," I called out to Dead Guy. "I'm guessing you've been out there all night?" I hadn't touched the body. Didn't need to, to know he was dead, but also, ewww. I may talk to ghosts, but that didn't mean I went around touching corpses.

His voice was muffled through the door. "It was late."

"How late?"

"After midnight." There was a sheepish tone to his voice, as if he'd realized knocking on my door in the middle of the night hadn't been the wisest of moves. Only he'd never knocked. Someone had stabbed him in the back before he'd reached my door. "I know, I know," he continued, "I should've waited until morning. I *really* wish I had now."

"I bet," I muttered, running my fingers through my messy bob and splashing water on my face again, rubbing at the smeared mascara under my eyes that I hadn't noticed on my first trip to the bathroom. Satisfied I wasn't going to look any better than I did right now, I flung open the door and eyeballed Dead Guy.

"What was so urgent you had to hire my services in the middle of the night?" Crossing to the night table, I picked up my phone and dialed while Dead Guy filled me in. I was hoping repeating the question would jog his memory.

"Something important," was his ambiguous reply. How very helpful. Not.

"You don't say." I tried one of those raised-eyebrow looks—the ones that let the person you're talking to know you're incredulous at their suggestion. Only I had yet to master individual control of my eyebrows, so instead, both brows shot into my hairline, and my look was one of surprise rather than disdain.

He shrugged. "It was a long shot."

The call connected. "Firefly Bay Police Department."

"Hi. This is Audrey Fitzgerald. I'm calling to report a murder."

# 2

"Is this a joke?" I eyed the takeout coffee cup Detective Kade Galloway held out to me.

"No. It's hot chocolate." He grinned, and my insides melted. *Captain Cowboy Hot Pants* was my main squeeze, and given my severe distrust of the police, that was saying something. But Galloway had not only wormed his way into my heart, he'd also been involved in the secret investigation bringing down the corrupt cops in the Firefly Bay PD. Now the bad guys were gone, and we had new blood in town, all on the right side of the law. I hoped.

"Tell me what happened," Galloway invited, standing with his arm around my shoulders while we both watched the activity unfolding on my front lawn.

"The official story is I came out this morning and found him like this." I waved an arm, almost spilling my hot chocolate.

"And the unofficial story?"

I glanced around to make sure we wouldn't be overheard then said out of the corner of my mouth, "Unofficially, his ghost told me he was out here."

"He's here now?" Galloway glanced around as if he could see Dead Guy's ghost for himself. I nodded.

"Have you asked him what happened?"

I snapped my head around in irritation. *Duh.*

Galloway barked out a laugh. "Of course you have. Well?"

"He doesn't know. He was coming to see me. Wanted to hire me, I assume, only he can't remember why. The next thing you know, he's got a knife in his back, and he's walking through walls."

"Identification says Dean Ward," Officer Noah Walsh called out from where he was kneeling next to the body holding Dead Guy's wallet in his hand.

"Ward?" Galloway arched a brow. "Is he from that brewery?"

Officer Walsh rifled through the wallet, pulling

out a business card. "Yep. Owns Moustache Craft Ales."

"That's the craft brewery on Bayview Street," Galloway said.

"Great burgers," I added.

"What's happened? Is that Dean Ward?" Ben appeared out of nowhere, making me jump.

"You know him?" I asked.

"Know *of* him," Ben said, crossing his arms over his chest and frowning. Yellow crime scene tape wrapped around bushes and trees, boots trampled across garden beds.

"Don't worry." I nudged him with my elbow, which achieved nothing other than making me stagger. "I'll fix the garden."

"It's not that." His frown deepened. "I'm more concerned with why he's here. On our front lawn."

"He was coming to see me. For a case."

Ben snorted. "Really? What?"

"Dunno. He has a case of ghost amnesia." A headache pounded at my temples, and I pinched the bridge of my nose. Turning to Galloway, I asked, "Do you have any Tylenol?"

"Probably got some in my car. Headache?"

"Mmmm."

"Hold tight. I'll go grab them. Just be careful,

Audrey, okay? You're talking to Ben… out loud." He reminded me my ghost-speaking abilities were meant to be secret. Usually, I was all over it, but my concentration was slipping. I really needed a coffee. Instead, I took a sip of hot chocolate and tried not to pull a face. It wasn't that I didn't like hot chocolate. I did. Mixed with coffee. Okay, fine, it's called café mocha, and I had a fierce craving for the brew.

"Delaney?" Dean caught sight of Ben and hurried over.

"What are you doing here, Ward?" Ben's voice had taken on a low, menacing tone, and I glanced at him in surprise. Did the two of them have history? Remembering Galloway's warning about being seen talking to ghosts, I pulled out my phone and pretended to take a call.

"Ben? What's going on?" I asked.

"He," Ben pointed an accusing finger at Dean, "is bad news. And he's brought trouble to your door, Fitz."

Dean snorted. "That's rich coming from you, a bent cop."

I sucked in a startled breath before leaping to Ben's defense. "He was not corrupt. He was framed." Heat washed up my face and burned, along with my temper.

"Easy, Fitz." But Ben wasn't looking at me. His eyes were glued to Dean, and his stance told me he was ready to spring into action at any moment, his weight on the balls of his feet, his hands clenched into fists. Could ghosts fight? I had an awful feeling I was about to find out.

"Ditto," I muttered. "Fill me in here. Why is he bad news?"

"Word around town is he has dealings with Arlie Roberts."

I sucked in a startled breath. Arlie Roberts *was* bad news. He and a gang of thugs ran the shady side of Firefly Bay. You didn't want to mess with them, and up until now, they'd always managed to avoid the long arm of the law. But with the cops most likely to accept bribes gone, Arlie Roberts and his mates were up a similar creek to mine. Were they the reason Dean was killed?

"Is this true?" I asked Dean, who wouldn't meet my eyes, instead keeping his glare on Ben.

"See?" Ben sneered, jerking his head. "He doesn't deny it. What was it, Ward? What were you fencing for Arlie? Money laundering? Cheap produce? Or was it the booze?"

Dean stiffened. "I brew my own ale, thank you very much!"

"Touch a nerve, did I?" Ben glanced at me. "I'd wager he was substituting some, if not all, of his self-brewed ales for cheap knock-off booze."

I didn't get a chance to reply. Dean launched himself at Ben, and the two of them went down in a tangle of limbs and fists, grunting and rolling across the lawn as both tried to get the upper hand. Sipping my hot chocolate, I watched until Galloway returned, holding out two painkillers.

"What's happening?" he asked, attempting to follow my gaze.

"Ben is sitting on Dean." Tossing the pills into my mouth, I gulped a mouthful of hot chocolate, choking and spluttering before I finally managed to swallow them.

"What do you mean, sitting on him?"

"They were fighting. And now Ben has Dean pinned to the lawn, knees holding his upper arms to the ground, sitting on him," I explained. Ben looked at me over his shoulder, grinning in triumph.

"Now what, big shot?" I asked.

"Everything okay here, Detective?" I hadn't noticed Officer Walsh approach and could have smacked myself in the head. I really needed to pay closer attention to what was going on around me if I wanted to keep my ghost-speaking abilities secret. *Only two more days, Fitz. You can do this.*

"Everything's fine, thanks, Officer," Galloway said, giving my shoulder a squeeze. "You may have heard that Audrey is on a caffeine-free kick? That has resulted in some unusual side effects."

"Ahhh." Officer Walsh nodded in apparent understanding. "Talking to herself more than usual?"

"Definitely."

"I am right here, you know!" I snapped, annoyed at the undercurrent of humor in the men's conversation.

"And I wouldn't have it any other way." Galloway dropped a kiss on my cheek in an attempt to pacify me. It totally worked.

"Any idea what Ward was doing on your front lawn?" Officer Walsh asked, diverting attention away from my current caffeine deprivation.

I shrugged. "No idea. He wasn't a client, although if he was coming to see me, I assume he wanted to hire me for something."

"Well, whatever it was, someone wanted him stopped."

I blinked in surprise. I hadn't thought of that. Dean was here to hire me—to investigate something, obviously, but he was killed before he could secure my services. Before he could tell me anything. Which meant that whatever it was, was big. Someone had wanted to stop him from blabbing to me. My eyes narrowed, and I turned to Galloway.

"I hear," I jerked my head sideways to indicate Ben, who was still sitting atop Dean, "that Dean had some underhand dealings with Arlie Roberts."

"Arlie Roberts, as in the Roberts gang?" Officer Walsh repeated, even though I'd directed my words to Galloway.

I nodded.

"Where did you hear that?" he pressed.

"Just around." No way I was telling him my dead best friend had just told me.

"Do you know what the dealings were?"

I shook my head. "No idea. Could be anything, really. Money laundering? Black market produce? Booze?" I echoed Ben's words.

"Walsh, go find Arlie and bring him in to the station to answer a few questions," Galloway instructed.

"Yes, sir." Officer Walsh hurried away, determination in every step.

"He's doing well, isn't he?" I watched the young officer as he climbed into his patrol car and waited for his partner to join him. I had a bit of a soft spot for Officer Noah Walsh. He reminded me of Ben when he'd first joined the force.

Galloway nodded. "Wants to sit his sergeant's exam soon."

"You think he's ready?" He seemed so... young.

"I do. He's smart. He can think on his feet. He's inquisitive and tenacious. A lot like someone else I know." He nudged me with his elbow, and I preened, standing taller and thrusting out my chest at the compliment. Then I took a mouthful of hot chocolate and dribbled it down my front.

Galloway barked out a laugh and ruffled my hair. "Don't ever change, Audrey. I love you just the way you are."

I snorted. "A drink-spilling, stained clothes-wearing, ghost-talking wreck?"

"A beautiful, sexy, drink-spilling, stained clothes-wearing, ghost-talking genius."

"Now you're just taking the—"

"Take the compliment, Fitz!" Ben called, climbing off Dean and hauling him to his feet. The two men stood side by side, dusting non-existent grass off themselves.

"Is this going to be a problem?" I eyeballed the pair of them. "Are you constantly going to be at each other's throats, or did that little rumble get it out of your system?"

Ben rolled his shoulders and slapped Dean on the back. "I'm good. You?"

Dean looked sheepish. "I'm good."

"Right. Now maybe we can get on with solving your murder."

## 3

"I can't believe he's gone! I loved him so much!" Leah Dunn wailed, great heaving sobs shaking her frame. Galloway and I looked at each other then back at Dean Ward's girlfriend of three years. I'd never witnessed such an outpouring of grief before. Sure, I'd seen people cry, but this? This was a whole other level.

"I knew she'd take it badly," Dean said somewhat smugly, as if his girlfriend's devastation was a good thing.

"I'm sorry for your loss," Galloway offered. The wailing stopped, and Leah blew her nose, loudly, into a tissue before raising red-rimmed eyes.

"It was that Eric Sullivan that did it." Her voice

was cold and brittle, her anguish betrayed by the small hiccup at the end.

"You know who killed your boyfriend?" I asked, eyebrows doing their thing, hanging out in my hairline.

She sniffed and nodded. "It was Sullivan. He was in the pub just the other night bragging about his stupid award. Deliberately riled Dean up, he did."

"What happened?" Galloway leaned forward, elbows on knees, face intent.

"Dean threw him out, of course. Told him he was barred and that *if you come around here again, I'll smash your head in.*"

Galloway and I exchanged a look. I don't know what he was thinking, but my immediate thought was *I need coffee*. The second was we needed to speak with Eric Sullivan, whoever the heck he was. But also, it sounded like Dean had threatened him, not the other way around.

"So, who's Eric Sullivan? And what award?" I asked.

Leah's blue eyes snapped to me. "He runs Firefly Bay Brewing Company. In fact, he and Dean started it together years ago, until Dean left to start his own business. The Moustache Craft Ale House. They've been in competition ever since. And Eric just won the Craft Ale of the Year award, something that Dean has been coveting ever since he struck out on his own."

"It's true," Dean said from behind me. "Never could crack it. But Eric won. Again. Second year in a row, and he couldn't stop from parading in to rub my face in it, dissing my pub, calling my menu *over-priced gastro garbage*."

"Right."

"How long have you known Dean?" Galloway asked Leah.

"We met when he was still working with Eric at Firefly Bay Brewing Company, just over three years ago. There was some big event on, I can't remember what it was now, but I'd landed a gig as a waitress, just for the night, mind you, but money is money, can't turn down a job. Shortly after that, he left and started Moustache Craft Ales and hired me as a bartender."

"Right. And how long have you been in a relationship?"

"About the same. I'd been there a week, learning the ropes and helping get everything set up. Then we had the big grand opening, and one thing led to another and well… here we are, three years later."

Dean sighed. "That was some party."

Leah cleared her throat and looked at me. "I'm sorry, but do you think you could get me some water?"

"Oh. Uh, sure." I stood and looked around the apartment she shared with Dean. "Kitchen that way?"

"Yes, just through there. Thank you."

Galloway sat with his head tilted to one side, and I paused as I squeezed past him, taken aback momentarily by his handsome good looks and magnetic presence. I cast a quick glance at Leah, who, if it weren't for the smudged mascara and red-tipped nose, I'd say was looking at him with the same appreciation. Was the request for water a ruse to get him alone?

Deciding my caffeine-deprived brain was working overtime in the wrong direction, I shrugged it off and continued on my way to the kitchen, which, like the rest of the apartment, was small. Its galley style served it well, and I didn't have far to search before I found a glass and held it under the faucet. As I turned to return to the living room, a photograph pinned to the refrigerator caught my attention, and I moved closer to get a better look.

Dean stood with his arm around a smiling Leah who was holding a tray of drinks. On the other side of her, another man stood with his arm around her as well. The three of them looked happy.

Returning to the living room, I caught Leah with her hand on Galloway's knee. I skidded to a halt and eyeballed her. Blonde and blue-eyed, taller than me, but I could take her. Narrowing my eyes, I shoved the water glass toward her, not caring that the sudden movement sloshed water over the rim.

"Thank you," she said, taking a sip then placing the glass on the coffee table.

"Who's the other guy in the photo on your fridge?" I asked, sitting back down on the sofa next to Galloway. He reached out and rested his hand on my thigh, giving it a reassuring squeeze. Leah's eyes followed his every move, and I shot her a look of warning. He was mine. I was also curious how she could be wailing her grief over her deceased boyfriend only minutes before making a move on mine.

"That's him. Sullivan."

"When was it taken?"

"That was the night we met. The event at the Firefly Bay Brewing Company."

"You all looked friendly enough."

"We were, then. But something changed after

that night, and Dean quit to start up his own pub, and he and Eric stopped talking for months."

"Why?" Galloway asked.

She shrugged. "Don't know." But her eyes darted away, and I knew she was lying. Something big went down between Dean and Eric, and Leah knew exactly what it was. Only she wasn't sharing. Didn't matter. I'd ask Dean once we were out of here.

"Why are you here anyway?" Her words were directed at me. "You're not the police. A private investigator, you said? Why? Are the police hiring out these days?"

"Actually, your boyfriend died on my front lawn. On his way to hire me. For what, I don't know. Do you?"

The color left her face, leaving her pale, then returned in a flood of red. Once again, her eyes darted away, and her hand reached out for her water. The glass shook as she picked it up.

Her eyes welled with tears. "Could we continue this another time? I'm not feeling very well. This has been a terrible shock."

"Of course. If you think of anything, any reason someone would want to harm Dean, please give me a call." Galloway placed a business card on the coffee table and stood.

Slapping my own card next to Galloway's, I said, "Ditto," and followed him out.

Once we were in the car, I turned to him. "I don't know about her. I got a distinct vibe."

"You think the tears were just for show?"

"Oh, I think the tears were real enough. But she's definitely lying about something." I didn't reveal my thoughts about her motives, not while Dean was around. For while her tears were real, I didn't think they were genuine. Leah Dunn was not as devastated at Dean's death as she tried to make out. I wanted to know why.

Galloway nodded. "That's what I think too."

"What?" Dean scoffed from the back seat. "You can't think Leah killed me. Why? It makes no sense. She's right. You need to go speak to Eric, though why he'd want to sink a knife in my back now, after all this time, is beyond me."

I swiveled in my seat to look at him. "What happened between the two of you?"

"Nothing."

I snorted. "Come on, I didn't come down in the last shower. You don't go from being friends, posing for photos together, to mortal enemies and throwing him out of your pub over nothing. Give."

Dean's shoulders reached his ears, and he turned his palms up. "Told you, I got nothing."

"You're lying." I knew it. He knew it. The smirk on his face told me he knew I knew and didn't care. "Fine, don't tell me. I'll go ask Eric."

"You do that. Won't do you any good."

"You know what? I'm starting to think you're not a very nice individual," I snapped.

"Isn't the first time I've heard that, sweetheart."

"Don't call me sweetheart!"

"Babe?" Galloway captured my flailing hand in his and drew my attention away from the annoying ghost in the back seat. "Everything okay?"

I deflated like a balloon with a slow leak. "I'm fine."

"Uh-oh," Dean chimed in from the back seat. "We all know what that means when a woman says she's fine."

"Will you just go away?" I pinched the bridge of my nose, my headache returning.

"I sincerely hope you're talking to Dean and not me," Galloway murmured. My head snapped up, and I wriggled across the parking brake to plant a kiss on his cheek in silent apology. "I never want you to go away."

Galloway turned his head, his lips meeting mine

in a kiss that sizzled. Dean made a kissing noise from the back seat, and I reluctantly pulled away, whispering against Galloway's mouth, "We have ghost company."

"To be continued," Galloway growled, pressing one last kiss on my lips before disengaging. Starting the car, we'd just pulled away when his phone rang.

"Galloway." He picked the call up via the car's Bluetooth.

"We've picked up Arlie Roberts," Officer Walsh's voice came over the speakers. "Did you want to interview him, or should I ask Detective McClain?"

Galloway nodded. "I'll be right there." Disconnecting the call, he turned the car in the direction of the Firefly Bay PD. I swiveled to look at Dean in the backseat. "Hear that? We're going to interview Arlie Roberts. Anything you want to tell us beforehand? Save a little time?"

"I've got nothing to say." Dean crossed his arms over his chest and mulishly pressed his lips together.

"Have it your way." I faced the front and studied my nails. "We'll find out soon enough. Detective Galloway here is the best. He'll have Roberts singing like a canary in no time." I caught the sideways glance Galloway shot my way and raised one shoulder. There was something about Dean Ward that I didn't trust. I got the same vibe from his girlfriend. He may not remember what he'd been doing on my front lawn, but he definitely knew Arlie Roberts and was no doubt up to his eyeballs in some sort of shady deal. I didn't know why he was so worried about keeping whatever it was a secret now. He was already dead. How much worse could it get?

At the station, it was business as usual. Desks took up most of the main room. A glass wall separated the public entrance and the administration area upfront. I headed toward the coffeepot while Galloway headed toward the interview rooms, Dean following.

"Hey Audrey, how's it going?" Sergeant Addison Young glanced up from where she was typing at her desk. "Hear you had a bit of excitement at your place this morning."

"Yeah, you could say that." I had the coffeepot in hand and was about to pour when I reluctantly remembered my bet with Amanda. No coffee. With an audible sigh, I returned the coffeepot and simply stood looking at it mournfully.

"How much longer?" Addison asked, coming to stand next to me, a comforting hand on my shoulder.

"Two days." May as well have been two years.

"You've got this. We're all backing you."

I eyeballed her. "How much did you put on me?"

She blinked innocently. "What do you mean?"

"Pft. I'm not that green. What's the bet? That I'll make it seven days without caffeine? Or that I'll cave, and Amanda will win?"

"Oh, hey Audrey. Two more days!" Officer Tom Collier gave me the thumbs up as he approached. I moved out of the way to give him access to the coffeepot.

"How much did you put down?" I asked him.

"Fifty on you to win," he said, pouring himself a cup of coffee then wafting it under my nose. "Want a sniff?"

Did I ever! I inhaled, the coffee-scented steam filling my sinuses. The fog permeating my brain lifted for a brief moment but quickly descended again when Tom removed the coffee from my vicinity. Probably for the best. I was practically drooling as it was.

"Did anyone bet against me?" I asked.

"Hell, no." Tom guffawed. "We all know you, Audrey Fitzgerald, and you are made of true grit. You've got this." I was humbled by their utter faith in me. Totally misplaced, of course, but now I knew they'd backed me, with money no less, I'd be a right heel if I stumbled at the last hurdle.

Right on cue, my phone buzzed with an incoming message from Amanda. *Don't forget Laura's baby shower is this afternoon.*

*I haven't forgotten,* I shot back. I had, but Amanda didn't need to know that. Laura was my sister who was heavily preggers with baby number two, and today was her baby shower. Not that she needed much—baby number one, Isabelle, was eighteen months old and Laura still had all her baby gear. I'd already picked up my gift and stashed it in the closet. A jumbo pack of diapers. Memorable? Not so much. Practical? Heck, yeah.

*What do you need me to bring?*

I frowned at the latest text from Amanda. Bring?

*Bring where?* I asked.

*To the baby shower, silly. At your house.*

Holy crap balls! I'd forgotten not only was it Laura's baby shower day, but I was also hosting it. At my house. The same house that had crime scene tape decorating the front garden.

"Addison, can you get Galloway to call me when he's done?" I nodded toward the interview rooms at the rear of the station. "Something's come up, and I've gotta run."

# 4

"Wilson, my man, you're getting five stars!"

"Thank you, Miss Audrey. I sure appreciate that. So does Bird."

I squinted at the bedraggled green and yellow budgie currently sitting on Wilson's shoulder, pecking at the stubble on the old man's cheek. I'd resorted to hiring an Uber when I realized I was stranded at the police station since I'd hitched a ride with Galloway earlier. Wilson had rolled up in his lime green sedan, wearing a fedora with what looked suspiciously like a bullet hole in it and a grin that hinted that this wrinkled old man had a life well-lived.

"Right." Flinging open the rear door, I retrieved

my shopping bags, cast a final look at the glow-in-the-dark spaceship ceiling stickers, and tumbled out of the car.

"Want a hand, Miss Audrey?" Wilson asked, dangling one arm out the open window, his nicotine-stained fingers drumming the paintwork as he watched me wrestle the five bags into submission.

"No thanks, I've got it," I puffed, clutching three bags in one hand, two in the other.

Wilson's phone dinged. "Gotta roll. Thanks for driving Uber today, Miss Audrey." He cocked his hat, hit reverse, and shot out of my driveway like a bat out of hell.

"Bye, Wilson. Bye, Bird." By the time the words had left my lips, Wilson was nothing but a spec of taillights at the end of the street. Hefting up the bags, I struggled down the path with my heavy load of party supplies.

My fingers were on fire by the time I reached the front door, with angry red welts marring my flesh. Dropping my load on the doormat, I unlocked the door, pulled out my phone, and dialed.

"Mom, I need help."

---

The party was in full swing when Ben and Dean appeared. And by full swing, I mean there were a dozen loud, giggly women sipping on champagne and playing baby shower games. The current game was where you blow up a balloon, shove it under your shirt, and then try and pop it by any means necessary. So far, they were stalled at step one, blowing up the balloon.

"I'm just stepping outside for some fresh air," I said into Laura's ear. "You okay here, need anything? More apple juice?"

Laura laughed at the antics of her friends and waved me away, "I'm all good, thanks, Sis." I turned away, but her hand suddenly reached out and clamped around my wrist. "Thanks for this. You've done a marvelous job, and I know it can't have been easy. You know, with your lack of coffee and all."

I turned back and hugged her. "Mom helped." Mom lived for this type of thing and had been thrilled when I'd called her. She'd come through my house like a tornado, throwing up decorations of blue and pink, dragging a massive bag of party game supplies with her. Turns out she'd been slowly building up a stash throughout Laura's pregnancy for this very occasion.

Removing myself from Laura's embrace, I caught Ben's eye and gestured toward the back deck. He followed, although while I went through the door, Ben strolled ever so casually through the glass.

"Party's a hit." Ben took a seat next to me on the edge of the deck.

I scuffed a toe in the grass. "Yep. Pretty much Mom's doing."

"You feel bad about that?" I didn't miss the note of surprise in his voice.

"Pft. No! I'm more than happy to take any help I can get. Plus, Mom was thrilled when I called. I get the feeling she was waiting for it."

Ben grinned. "I think you're right."

"Why are you sitting around here, throwing parties of all things, when you should be out there solving my murder?" Dean joined us, his accusing tone grating on my nerves. I was starting to not like this ghost very much.

"Because I have obligations other than you," I snapped. It wasn't like I'd bailed on Dean's murder investigation. I'd just paused it. Once the baby shower was over, I'd head out. I wanted to talk to Eric Sullivan. And scope out Moustache Craft Ales. I already had a hinky feeling about Dean's girlfriend,

Leah. I was curious what a little more poking would uncover.

"Why don't you tell me something helpful for a change? What were your dealings with Arlie Roberts?"

Dean stiffened, his eyes narrowing. A sheen appeared across his top lip. Turning to Ben, I whispered, "Can ghosts sweat?"

"No."

I pointed at the moisture beading on Dean's pale skin. "Then why is he sweating?"

Ben stood and approached the other ghost. "Interesting," he murmured, leaning in close to examine the perspiration in question.

"Very." The mere mention of Arlie Roberts was enough to have Dean breaking out in an incorporeal sweat. "Come on, Dean, you may as well spill. I'm going to find out anyway. Let's just expedite the whole process and cut to the chase. You don't owe Arlie anything now. He can't hurt you—you're already dead. Unless he's the one who did the killing?"

He crumpled like one of the deflated balloons inside. His shoulders rolled in, his arms hung limp, his lips turned down at the corners. "I did something stupid," he whispered.

Leaning in closer, I urged him on. "What?"

His eyes met mine, and I saw the defeat in them. Despite not liking the man very much, my heart went out to him. Why was I such a sucker for puppy dog eyes?

"I haven't produced any decent ale in months. Initially, it was one bad batch, but that was enough to set me back significantly. I was in a pinch, and Arlie was in the right place at the right time, offering me up a deal. I took it. I told you, I was desperate. But it was meant to be a one-time thing, not ongoing."

"He loaned you cash?" Ben asked, but Dean shook his head.

"You weren't wrong earlier. Watered down booze."

"Why didn't you stop then?" I asked.

"Because Arlie wouldn't let me. I was in over my head and couldn't get out. If I told the cops, I'd lose my license. The pub and Leah? They are my life... I was scared I'd lose them both."

Hands on his hips, Ben barked out a harsh laugh. "You really are a moron. Dude, you're dead. And chances are it was Arlie Roberts who plunged that knife in your back to stop you from squealing."

"Is that why you were coming to see me? To use

me to try and get you out of your underhanded deal with Arlie?" A shiver danced up my spine at the trouble Dean had brought to my door. Seemed Ben was connecting the dots too, for a flash of light burned through his visage, like his aura had flared for the briefest of moments, indicating his rage.

He grabbed Dean's shirt in his fist and hauled him forward until they were nose to nose. "You brought your seedy problems to her door," he spat, "and that is not acceptable."

Dean held out his arms in a supplicating gesture. "Hey, I told you, I can't remember why I was coming here, why I wanted to hire her." Then his demeanor changed. The beaten, downtrodden man was replaced with the sneering, dishonorable one. "Seems to me you have the hots for your little human friend here, Delaney. What do you do when she's not looking, hmm? Sneak a peek in the shower? A little touch while she's sleeping?" He jerked out of Ben's grip, his lip curled in a leer as his eyes slid over my body.

Ew. This guy really was a slimeball.

"Back off," Ben growled, and I glanced at him out of the corner of my eye. "You two aren't going to kick off again, are you?" Stupid question. Ben practically vibrated with anger, and Dean was intentionally provoking him.

Dean planted his feet and backwards-waved to Ben. "Come on, bacon. Think you can take me?"

"Bacon?" I winced at the insult while Ben shot forward and into Dean's face.

Well, not literally, that would have been too weird, but they were inches apart when Ben said, "Want your butt kicked twice in one day? Happy to oblige."

*Here we go again.* The two men went down in a tangle of limbs, rolling across the lawn accompanied by the sound of punches being thrown and grunts when they connected. Rolling my eyes, I decided I didn't need to witness this and got up, ready to go back inside, when something caught my eye. Beneath the deck, crouched low, were Bandit and Thor.

"Guys?" I crouched on the lawn and peered at them. "What's up?"

"Thor is teaching me," Bandit replied in her chirpy voice then motioned with her paw for me to move over so she could see the fight.

"Teaching you what?" I had a sneaking suspicion I knew precisely what it was, and Thor confirmed it.

"The art of the deal," he said.

"Deal? As in bet? As in gamble?"

"Precisely."

"Thor. What exactly are you betting on? Are you taking advantage of Bandit's good nature? You know she doesn't understand these things."

"Oh, no, it's okay, Audrey," Bandit assured me. "Thor is my friend. He promised he wouldn't take my fleece!"

I narrowed my eyes and pinned Thor with a glare. "Did you threaten to fleece her, Thor?"

His nose lifted in the air. "I did no such thing. Our dealings are purely in kibble."

Oh, good Lord. My cat was placing bets with my raccoon to win her share of kibble. I *knew* this diet was a bad idea. Unfortunately for Thor, the vet insisted.

"Thor, Bandit, listen up." I snapped my fingers to get both their attention. "No more bets. No more gambling. This ends now."

"But—" Thor protested, and I raised a finger to silence him.

"It ends now. Bandit is entitled to her own food. It's not like you're starving, Thor."

"But I am! I'm wasting away, a mere shell of my former self," he wailed.

"It's okay, Thor, you can have my kibble," Bandit generously offered.

I sighed. Bandit was the most generous raccoon, and her heart was in the right place. Sadly, Thor's was in his stomach.

"That won't be necessary, Bandit, but thank you for the offer. You will each continue to receive your own measured portion of kibble. There will be no swapping, no dealing, no stealing. Am I understood?"

There was a three-second pause before Thor begrudgingly grumbled, "Understood."

"Understood," Bandit repeated, though I doubted she understood at all. She loved Thor to pieces and would do anything for him, including starve herself.

Shaking my head, I grinned. "The party's almost over. If you promise to follow the food situation rules, I'll give you a treat from the leftovers. One treat. Each."

Thor brightened considerably and promised with a heartfelt nod of his head. Bandit mimicked him, and I laughed, straightening to stand when I froze. Standing on the deck was Amanda. Watching me. Talking to my pets.

"It's almost as if you can understand them." She took a sip of champagne.

"I can. In my own way." I watched her cautiously. Amanda was forever trying to fix me, my clumsiness, my quirkiness. But I'd noticed lately that she'd gotten really intense about it. So intense that it was driving a wedge between us, and I didn't want that. She was my brother's wife, and I didn't want a rift in the family, but I also didn't want Amanda's constant pressure, the insistence that there was something wrong with me.

"Maybe an MRI is in order."

"What?" I blinked. Had I heard her right? She wanted my brain scanned?

The back door slid open, and Laura waddled out. "Everything okay?" Her eyes darted from me to Amanda and back again.

"Yeah, sure. Amanda was just saying she thinks I need an MRI." I huffed, annoyed all over again.

"Really?" Laura's eyebrows rose, and she turned to Amanda. "Why?"

"Audrey displays several unique traits, aside from her inherent clumsiness. The way she talks to her animals, for instance. I'm not sure that's normal."

"But you don't have any pets, do you, Amanda?" Laura said. "So, how would you know if it's normal for someone to talk to their pets or not? These are merely your own observations from your own perspective on life. It's hardly fair for you to judge Audrey on what you perceive to be... normal."

I nodded in silent agreement. Laura had said it better than I ever could. Amanda cocked her head and considered what Laura had said.

"Mmm. Perhaps." She finally conceded.

Laura turned her back to Amanda and grinned at me. "Thanks for an awesome party, Sis. I've had a brilliant time, but I'm going to head off. Baby number two is demanding I take a nap."

I affectionally rubbed her belly. "What baby number two wants, baby gets." We were in the final weeks of Laura's pregnancy, and realistically the baby could arrive at any time. I was bursting with excitement and couldn't wait to meet my new niece or nephew.

"I'll stay and help clean up," Amanda declared, following us inside where the party was wrapping up.

"Not necessary." I tripped over the threshold and stumbled inside.

It really wasn't. Mom was on it. She zipped around like a demon, trash bag in hand, scooping up exploded pieces of balloon, empty paper plates and cups, and making short work of it.

She glanced up at us. "Oh good, you're here.

Amanda, start carrying the presents out to the car, will you?"

"Certainly."

"Thanks," I mouthed to Mom while I acted the hostess and thanked everyone for coming. Within half an hour, my house was empty once more. Despite the air smelling distinctly of baby powder, you'd never know the chaos that had ensued when a bunch of women got together over a baby.

I glanced at my smartwatch—I was on the third replacement. Don't ask. Just gone six-thirty, a perfect time to visit Firefly Bay Brewing Company and chat with Eric Sullivan.

*Fancy a hot date?* I texted Galloway.

*Always,* he shot back.

# 5

What I really wanted was the sprucehead stout with chocolate and coffee undertones. Pairs well with a burger, the hipster bartender with his oiled beard told us. But a bet was a bet, and I was determined to win. No caffeine. Not even in beer. Instead, I ordered the twin-screw pale ale and a pizza. Galloway chose the same.

"So." I took a sip of my brew and glanced around the interior of the Firefly Bay Brewing Company. It was all black steel, dark rustic wood, and a lot of plants in tins. There were two huge vats on display, and the smell of hops was in the air. While the building itself was old, it had been renovated into a very hipster, modern, and in vogue space with original stone walls. The beer tasted good too. "Did you get anything from Arlie Roberts?"

Galloway chuckled and took a mouthful of his own drink, eyeing me over the rim of the glass. "I suspect you already know, but I'll humor you."

My eyes rounded, and I placed my glass on the table with a thunk. "Arlie squealed?"

"Hardly." Galloway snorted. "But a search warrant revealed over a dozen barrels of beer in his back shed."

"Ahhh." I nodded. "The beer he was selling to Dean to water down the brew at Moustache Craft Ales."

"Is that what he told you?"

"Mmhmm. He also said that he was in over his head and didn't know how to get out. Do you think Arlie killed him?"

"At first glance, that seems possible but think about it. If Arlie has a lucrative deal going on with Ward, he's not going to let that go easily."

"But Dean wanted out. He was coming to me for help."

Galloway was already shaking his head. "Arlie is not going to kill his cash cow. He'd have been better off killing you." At my look of utter horror,

Galloway quickly continued, “Plus, murder is not Arlie’s style. He’s more threats and extortion.”

“So, you *don’t* think Arlie is the killer?”

“No, I don’t. It doesn’t make sense. Arlie isn’t stupid. He knows how to cover his tracks. Even if he was the killer, I find it highly doubtful he’d leave Ward’s body out in the open like that. He’d have disposed of it, made it so Dean Ward simply disappeared.”

“You’re right. Killing Dean on my front lawn and leaving the body there, with the knife in situ, is a sure-fire way to attract the police's attention. And attracting the attention of the police wouldn’t be high on Arlie’s agenda, I’m sure.”

A booming voice interrupted us. “Good evening. Hope you folks are enjoying your ales.” I recognized the man standing by our table immediately. Eric Sullivan. Owner of the Firefly Bay Brewing Company and Dean’s competition. A little shorter than Dean, a little wider, with an excellent start to a beer belly, but the same sprinkling of grays through his hair.

“We are, thank you,” Galloway replied.

“I hope you don’t mind me interrupting, but I recognized you as one of Firefly’s finest…” He trailed off, looking at Galloway hopefully.

Galloway took the hint. "Detective Kade Galloway." Standing up, he offered his hand. The two men shook in that manly way they do, sizing each other up while simultaneously squeezing the ever-living daylights out of each other's fingers.

Clearing my throat, I stood too. "Audrey Fitzgerald, private investigator." I held out my hand.

Surprise flashed across Eric's face, and he released Galloway's hand to seize mine. "You're a PI?"

"I am." I retrieved my hand and surreptitiously wiped my palm on my thigh. Eric Sullivan had clammy palms. Not only gross but I was curious as to why. Did he have something to hide? But then, he'd approached us! I really needed a shot of caffeine to get my thinking machine back in working order.

"Please, join us for a minute." Galloway indicated an empty seat at our table. "We have a few questions."

Eric sat, clasping his hands together and resting them on the tabletop. "Official police business, huh?" he joked.

"Actually, I'm off duty, but since I'm here and you're here…"

"Happy to help in any way I can." Eric smiled briefly. "I'm guessing this is about Dean?"

"You two were close once." I propped my elbows on the table and leaned in.

"He was my best friend. We started this place together." Eric waved a hand around. "Life was good."

"Then Dean left to start up Moustache Craft Ales," Galloway cut in.

"Why did he leave?" I added.

Eric grimaced. "We worked well together because we're both competitive, and we played off each other, pushed each other. I'd create a new ale recipe, and Dean immediately had to out-do it, that sort of thing." He leaned back in his chair, his fingers fiddling with a coaster. "But Dean was competitive over everything. And he took it too far."

An image of Dean, Leah, and Eric standing with their arms around each other beaming into the camera flashed through my brain. "Leah. You fell out over a woman."

Eric blew out a breath. "I met Leah first, but as soon as I mentioned to Dean that I fancied her? He immediately went over and made a move. And it worked. I tried to get over it, but… I don't know, it was like Dean got enjoyment out of rubbing my face in it, and things started to get really unpleasant at work. So, I bought him out and dissolved the partnership."

"It was you who instigated it? You ended the partnership?" Galloway asked.

"Oh, I know Dean was telling everyone that it was his decision to leave, that he wanted to set up shop on his own. But that wasn't how it came about."

Interesting. "Did Leah know about any of this?"

Eric shifted uncomfortably in his seat, and a flush of color bloomed across his cheeks. "She'd have had to be deaf and blind not to. Dean kept taunting me with their relationship right here in the bar. He'd say stuff like, *Leah, my love, you know that Eric had the hots for you, babe? But the best man won, isn't that right, Eric?* It was downright awkward for everyone. Dean just wouldn't leave it alone."

What a douche. It confirmed my opinion that Dean Ward really wasn't a very nice man. Thankfully his ghost hadn't followed us here tonight. The last I'd seen of him was when he and Ben tussled on the back lawn. Which wasn't like Ben at all. He wasn't a violent man, but this was the second altercation he'd had with Dean in a short amount of time. Again, I wondered why that was. What was it about Dean Ward that set Ben off?

Galloway placed his hand on mine on the tabletop, drawing my attention. The soft slide of his fingertips across the back of my hand sent a delightful spark of heat up my arm, and I grinned, turning my hand palm up and interlocking my fingers with his.

Eric didn't miss the gesture. "You two are together?"

"He's my boyfriend," I said proudly, as if I were ten years old and staking my claim on the playground. Galloway grinned, then winked, and I melted. He could turn me on by merely breathing. It should have been embarrassing. It wasn't.

"That's wonderful. You make a lovely couple." Eric smiled wistfully, then his attention was taken by something behind my shoulder. "If you'll excuse me, my daughter has just arrived."

Daughter? I swiveled in my seat so fast I almost fell off. I watched as Eric approached a young woman dressed in a short plaid skirt, white T-shirt, long hair that swung in a black waterfall to her waist, and black lipstick. I blinked. I wasn't quite sure what her style was, but she carried it off beautifully. I sighed, and Galloway squeezed my hand.

"Don't do that," he murmured.

"Do what?" I turned back to him as Eric and his daughter embraced.

"Compare yourself and then find yourself lacking. You are the most beautiful, compassionate, desirable woman I've ever met, and if you could only see what I see..."

I blinked. Then blinked again.

"I see dead people."

Galloway threw back his head and laughed, but I couldn't crack a smile.

"Trust you to ruin a moment, Fitz," he teased.

"No." I dropped my voice to a whisper. "I didn't mean that to be a corny line from some movie." I dragged in a deep breath. "I heard what you said, and I love you for it. But..." I shifted my gaze from his alluring gray eyes to the trio of dark, ominous spirits hovering on the far side of the room. They weren't like any ghost I'd seen before. These guys were almost shapeless, more dark shadows, hovering above the ground with swirls of black fog rolling over them and pooling on the floor.

Galloway followed my gaze. "What is it? Is Ward here?"

I shook my head, unable to speak. "Not Ward," I eventually squeaked out.

"Who? Has someone else died?" I heard the urgency in his voice but couldn't tear my attention away from the spirits as they slowly made their way across the room. I felt them as they moved behind us, icy tendrils brushing against my spine causing me to stiffen and sit ramrod straight, not relaxing until they'd passed, taking their icky juju vibe with them.

"Audrey?" Galloway prompted.

I slumped back in my seat, blowing out a breath.

"What happened?" he asked.

"There were... I don't think I can call them ghosts. They didn't really have a form, not like Ben and the others, who appear to me as exact replicas of their human selves. These were more like what I'd imagine a spirit to be. A spooky, scary spirit. The ones that haunt you, the ones that make things go bump in the night. The ones that do bad things."

"Shit." Galloway's brows pulled together in concern.

"Exactly."

"Do you want to leave?"

I glanced over my shoulder to catch the spirits disappearing through the wall. "No need. They've gone now."

"Do you think they're attached to this building? Old ghosts that have been here so long they've changed into something else?"

I shrugged. "Possibly? This building is old, definitely. I'll have to do some research, see if anyone died here." Out the corner of my eye, I saw a waitress approaching. "Pizza's here." I plastered a fake smile on my face and pushed down the apprehension building within. I had no idea what the floating creatures were. But I sensed them. The darkness. The despair. They either caused it or fed off it. I wasn't sure which. All I knew was I was not a fan.

# 6

"We've had the best. Now let's try the rest!" I chortled, leaning heavily on Galloway's arm as we left Firefly Bay Brewing Company.

"Your liver is going to be so grateful when you start drinking coffee again," Galloway teased, steering my slightly inebriated self to his car in the parking lot.

"Right?" I grinned happily. Amanda thought she could break me, break my addiction, but the truth was, I was well aware of my reliance on coffee, and I had no intentions of quitting. This was just a stupid bet agreed to in the heat of the moment and an important life lesson for moi. *Do not let Amanda rile you.* As soon as the words agreeing to give up coffee had left my mouth and that flash of triumph had shot across her face, I knew she'd played me. Played me good.

"But this time, I have a new strategy," I said aloud, allowing Galloway to settle me into the passenger seat.

"What's that, babe? Strategy for what?" Before I could answer, he shut the door, so I waited for him to round the hood and slide behind the wheel.

"Amanda."

"A strategy for Amanda? Do tell."

"My strategy is no strategy. Do not engage."

"You know, that's the best idea I've ever heard from you." He winked and started the car. "You sure you want to go to Moustache Craft Ales tonight? Would you rather go home?"

I snorted. "The night is still young! But seriously," I sobered slightly, "I want to check out Moustachios and get a feel for the place, the staff, taste the beer… although I doubt I'd taste much of a difference after those two ales at Fireflies."

"Moustachios?" Galloway laughed.

"Well, they all have such long and ludicrous names," I complained. "There should be a law—if you're selling alcohol, keep your name short and sweet so your clientele can say it when they're drunk."

"There's a marketing angle I bet no one has considered."

"Maybe I should go into marketing," I mused.

"What, and leave sleuthing behind?" Galloway gasped with mock surprise. "You'd never last."

"You're right. I'm too good a PI to give it up."

Galloway reached out and patted my knee. "Never doubt it."

Moustache Craft Ales was same, same, but different. It definitely had the hipster-type vibe, but there were no vats to be seen. I sniffed the air. No hops either. But there was music, and it was loud, most likely due to the younger crowd.

"Do you think they brew their beer off-site?" I shouted at Galloway. That would make sense considering Dean had been substituting his own brew for God only knows what beverage Arlie had supplied.

"I'm not seeing any equipment here," he agreed as we made our way to the bar.

"What can I get you?" A twelve-year-old with an incredibly deep voice asked from behind the bar.

"Is he old enough to serve alcohol?" I whispered out of the corner of my mouth. Seems my whisper was louder than anticipated, for the child in question threw back his head and laughed.

"Not the first time I've heard that, ma'am. I can assure you, I'm old enough. I'm twenty-two." Before I could stop him, he whipped out his driver's license and shoved it in my face. I focused my eyes and read the name, Jay Byrne.

Galloway glanced at the license then at Jay. "What would you recommend, Jay?"

"First-timers?" Jay asked.

I nodded.

"In that case, I'd suggest our copper house ale. It has roasted malt notes and middle-of-the-road balanced flavor."

"Sounds good." I'd agree to anything at this point. I had no idea what roasted malt tasted like but wasn't averse to finding out.

Jay expertly poured our drinks while Galloway casually inquired how long he'd been working for Dean.

"Since he opened," Jay said.

"Must have been disappointing this place didn't win the Craft Ale of the Year award," I said.

Jay rolled his eyes. "Dean seemed to think we were in with a chance."

"You weren't so sure?"

"I guess? But the fact is that Eric has more money to invest in his business, experiment with new recipes, and expand—he's trialing a cider now. Dean, well, not to speak ill of the dead or anything, and he was my boss and all, but Dean spent too much time with his head in the clouds and not enough time getting down to business." Jay slid my drink toward me. "On the house."

"Thanks." I took a sip. It was nice. Not outstanding or incredible or award-wining. But okay.

"We understand there's bad blood between Eric and Dean. Know anything about that?" Galloway asked.

Jay barked out a derisive laugh. "You couldn't miss it. Dean was always niggling at Eric, either to his face or behind his back."

Galloway and I glanced at each other. Nothing new there.

"But I did happen to see the two of them arguing a couple of days ago," Jay added.

"Was that when Eric was in here to gloat about winning the award?"

Jay frowned. "Err, no, I'm not sure that happened. Eric dropped in, sure, but there was no gloating that I could see. No mention of the award. All I know is that I heard Dean say, *you owe me.*"

"What did Eric say?"

"*I owe you nothing.* And then he left. Dean sulked in his office for hours after that."

Jay got called away to serve another customer while Galloway and I enjoyed our beer and contemplated the case. So, Leah and Dean had lied about how the disagreement with Eric had gone down. Dean hadn't thrown Eric out. Eric had left under his own volition.

"The bad blood between Eric and Dean runs pretty deep." I fiddled with a coaster. "Deep enough to kill?"

"I'm not seeing the motive," Galloway admitted. "Why would Eric kill Dean? The Firefly Bay Brewing Company is doing well. It's winning awards. He's coming out top dog over Mustache Craft Ales. Then there are Dean's dealings with Arlie and the knock-off alcohol. Eric didn't need to kill Dean to come out on top business-wise. The more we dig, the more it appears Dean was self-imploding."

"What about Leah? Eric says she's what caused the rift in the first place."

"True, but that wasn't Leah's fault or doing. It was Dean. Eric confided to his friend that he liked her, and then Dean, knowing full well his best friend had feelings for her, went and asked her out. Plus, that was three years ago. Why wait this long to do something about it?" Galloway pointed out.

"You're right. As far as motives go, it's pretty flimsy."

"But a business rival does make a good suspect. On paper, at least."

Resting my chin on my hand, I pondered the murder of Dean Ward. So far, I had three suspects. The girlfriend, Leah Dunn. The ex-business partner, Eric Sullivan. And Arlie Roberts, distributor of illegal booze and generally an overall shady character.

Their motives were pretty flimsy too. Leah had no cause to want her boyfriend dead—not that I'd found anyway. It was doubtful Eric had killed him after a three-year feud. And Arlie would be cutting off a cash supply by killing him.

"Dean still can't remember why he was coming to see you?" Galloway asked, his bar stool so close our thighs touched, distracting me with his warmth.

"No." I pouted. Admittedly it would have been so much easier if we had that piece of the puzzle, but then again, it was all part of solving the mystery, connecting the dots, revealing clues until we got to the truth. I snapped my head around and pinned Galloway with a look.

"What?" He laughed, jerking back a little at the ferocity in my gaze.

I blinked. "Sorry. I just had a thought."

"Okay..."

"I'm a PI."

"I know."

"Most people hire me for things like, oh you know, *cheating spouses*."

Galloway slowly nodded his head. "You think maybe Dean thought Leah was cheating and wanted to know for sure?"

"It's plausible. But did she kill him? I'm not sure. I mean, I think it's pretty extreme to stab a guy in the back to stop him from finding out you're cheating on him."

"We keep circling back to that. Maybe the reason he was hiring you and the reason he was killed were two different things and not connected at all?"

I slumped on the bar, resting my forehead against the hard surface. "Gah," I grumbled. Galloway massaged my neck, his fingers sure and knowing, and my stress melted away with his expert touch. I sighed, then murmured, "I'm pretty sure I'm drooling on this bar."

Galloway laughed and pulled me upright. "How about I get you home, hmm? Let's sleep on it."

"Going home sounds great, but I wasn't planning on sleeping." I winked and slid my arms around his waist, pressing myself against him.

"Neither was I, Fitz." He squeezed my butt, waved goodbye to Jay, and we headed out. I only hoped I didn't fall asleep in the car as I had plans for Kade Galloway tonight, and they required staying awake.

# 7

"Babe." A gentle nudge prodded me toward wakefulness. I did not want to go. "Nooooo." I was having another one of those dreams. Coffee nirvana. I was in a tub of it, my back and shoulders were being massaged with a divine coffee scrub, and the scent of it was all around me. I never wanted to leave.

"Babe, you fell asleep at your desk. Again."

I blinked my eyes open, the dream dissipating, leaving behind a yearning that I'd kill for. Well, almost kill for. The massaging had been real though. Galloway was gently kneading my shoulders, easing me to wakefulness as my upper body lay slumped across my desk. Struggling into a sitting position, I winced at the crick in my neck.

"What time did you come down?" Galloway moved his fingers to my neck, found the spot, and proceeded to work the knots out.

"About three. I woke up and couldn't get back to sleep, so I figured I may as well get some work done."

"And? Any progress?"

I stretched and yawned, hitting Galloway with a face full of morning breath before clamping a hand over my mouth and apologizing. He waved away my apology with a kiss on the cheek before straightening and heading toward the door, calling over his shoulder, "Green tea?"

"Wash your mouth out." I scowled. "I'll take decaf." A poor substitute if ever there was one.

"One more day." Galloway disappeared from view to prepare our morning beverages while I shuffled off to use the bathroom. We met back in my office minutes later.

I pointed to my computer screen, where a crime scene board was displayed. "I've done some digging."

"And?"

"Two things." I held up a finger. "First, it seems Dean was on the brink of bankruptcy." I knew the police would discover this information for themselves, but all the better if I could hurry things along.

"Probably why he got involved with Arlie Roberts. Desperate times call for desperate measures. Trying to save his business by any means necessary."

"And Jay said to us that Dean didn't seem to have much of a head for business. I'm paraphrasing, of course."

"Makes sense. Running a business is hard. Apparently, Dean didn't have the same keen business sense as Eric. What else did you find?"

"I was going over his phone records, and there was one pay-as-you-go number that he called a couple of days ago. It only lasted a few seconds."

Galloway took a mouthful of his tea while I sipped on my decaf and pretended it was *real* coffee. I let him mull over my discoveries in silence.

"Is Dean here now?" he eventually asked.

"Nope. Ben usually stays out all night, watching Netflix or whatever with his insomniac friends. I don't know where Dean is. Probably not with Ben, though. The two of them do not get along." I told Galloway of the second fight between the ghosts.

"That's not like Ben."

My thoughts exactly. "Ben thought Dean was coming to see me because of Arlie. Maybe Dean thought I could do something about his situation?"

Galloway's brows pulled low. "That's not what PI's do."

"Now you sound all protective like Ben. We keep coming back to why Dean wanted to hire me. Didn't we agree last night to take that out of the equation? What if Dean's body was found somewhere else? What if it had nothing to do with me at all?"

"You're right. Your involvement is clouding our judgment."

"Especially as I don't know what my involvement is. Or was. Or potentially was."

Galloway peered at the list of suspects on my screen. He jabbed at the monitor with a finger. "You like Eric Sullivan for this?"

I shrugged. "I think we could give him a closer look. He's Dean's ex-business partner. He just won an award that Dean coveted. Jay saw the two of them arguing. It seems to me the bad blood between them has never been resolved. Maybe Eric wanted to be done with it once and for all, and the only way to get Dean to leave him alone was to kill him." For there was one thing I realized about Dean Ward. He was a vindictive man who was pretty loose with the truth. Did he push Eric too far?

"Okay, you look into Eric, and keep me posted.

I'm still working on the Arlie Roberts angle. The interview yesterday got us enough for a search warrant."

I frowned in confusion. "I thought you said you didn't think Arlie was our killer?"

"I don't. But he's still a criminal, and if we can get him on some other charge, good. If we can get him on something big that will dismantle his gang, even better."

"By good, you're not just talking illegal booze, are you?"

"By big, I mean guns and drugs. Arlie may not be our killer, but one of his men could be. I'm casting the net wide on this one."

I stood and looped my arms around Galloway's neck. "Please be careful."

He dropped a kiss on my lips. "Always."

I heard the cat flap bang against the window, followed by the thundering of furry paws. "He's up, he's up!" Bandit chortled, skidding into the office to stand on her hind legs and grab at Galloway's thigh.

"Good morning, Bandit." Galloway scooped up the raccoon and cuddled her in his arms, ruffling her fur.

"I love you!" Bandit declared, burrowing her face

into the soft spot between Galloway's neck and shoulder. "Love, love, love."

Galloway looked at me over the chittering raccoon's head, one brow raised.

"She's saying she loves you," I translated.

Galloway kissed her head and said, "I love you too, Bandit," before setting her on the floor.

Thor appeared in the doorway. "Is breakfast ready?" he demanded, and I burst out laughing.

"What?" Galloway and Thor said in unison.

Shaking my head, I explained, "Bandit comes running in for love and affection. You saunter in for food."

"I love food," Thor said simply.

"Come on, Thor, buddy. I'll get you some kibble before I go." Galloway scooped up the massive gray ball of fluff and scratched behind his ears as he carried him to the kitchen, Bandit at his heels. I could hear the purring from my office. Thor may love food, but he loved Galloway just as much.

After the animals were fed and Galloway was farewelled with a long, heartfelt kiss, I headed upstairs to shower. The shower was my thinking place, and as I stood under the hot spray, I let my mind wander. After touching on annoying subjects like Amanda and our stupid bet and briefly pondering why she hadn't called me at six a.m. this morning like she usually did, it meandered onto the subject of Leah Dunn. Leah, who was distraught at the news of her boyfriend's death, yet as soon as I was out of the room, appeared to make a move on my man.

Although, to be fair, that may have been my caffeine-deprived imagination making mountains out of molehills. Still, I couldn't help but circle back to why Dean was coming to see me—despite telling Galloway I wasn't pursuing that line of inquiry, it seems I couldn't let it go.

Stepping out of the shower, I dried off and dressed in denim cut-off shorts and a T-shirt, slipped my feet into canvas flats, and headed out, returning five minutes later to grab my phone before heading out for real. My smartwatch, I soon discovered, was dead yet again. Why I kept replacing these things was beyond me. I'd broken two and kept forgetting to charge the third. For a device that was supposed to make my life easier, it wasn't. I took it off, tossed it in my bag, and set a reminder on my phone to charge the smartwatch when I got home.

I pulled up in front of Leah's apartment just in time to catch her leaving. My timing couldn't have been more perfect. I followed her black Mazda to the parking lot of Moustache Craft Ales. No surprise, really, considering she worked there. I guessed she was managing the place now Dean was dead.

A light bulb went off in my head. Was that motive for murder? Did Leah want Moustache Craft Ales to herself? But surely she knew Dean was about to go bankrupt and lose it all? Which didn't make it much of a motive. Unless… I tapped my top lip. Unless Leah had money and was waiting to snatch Moustache Craft Ales at a bargain-basement price. I made a mental note to do a full financial check on Leah.

Parking on the street with a full view of the pub, I settled in. It was early, the pub was closed, but I figured there was plenty of work to be done in running a place like this. Cleaning. Re-stocking. Paperwork. Plus, with Dean dead, they were down a team member, which was probably why Leah was there before opening.

Absolutely nothing transpired for the next two hours, but then, just before eleven, action! Jay arrived for his shift. Then another staff member I didn't recognize. And another. Moustache Craft Ales was open for business. Patrons began to drift in. I assumed they were here for an early lunch, but I guess they could have been day drinkers. I wasn't here to judge.

I'd brought my binoculars with me, compact and discreet and really good for stakeouts, and they paid off when the side door opened and Jay stepped outside. He stood for a moment, eyes scanning the parking lot, nodded to himself, then strode toward a small red car I'd seen drive in a few minutes earlier. The window of the car rolled down, and an arm appeared. Whoever was in the car exchanged something with Jay, and my mind immediately jumped to one conclusion. Drugs.

My binoculars confirmed it. Jay slipped a tiny plastic bag from his pocket, handed it to the person in the car, and then shoved what appeared to be a couple of bills into his back pocket. He glanced around to make sure he hadn't been seen then hightailed it back inside.

The window rolled up on the car before I could get a look inside, and with its dark tint, I couldn't make out the shadowy figure behind the wheel. The vehicle was parallel to me, the plates hidden from view, but all I had to do was wait. I'd grab them when the car left, which was now!

My heart raced as I followed its progress with my binoculars, watched it traverse the parking lot, getting ready to pull out onto the street, any second now, and I'd see the plate. *Remember the number, remember the number,* I chanted silently.

And just as it exited the parking lot, a truck drove past, obscuring my view. By the time the truck had passed, the little red car was gone.

"Damn, damn, damn," I cussed, slapping the steering wheel. But maybe all was not lost. Maybe I could follow it? Tossing my binoculars on the passenger seat, I started the engine, flicked on my turn signal, and was about to pull away in hot pursuit when another car caught my eye. A green Land Rover with personalized plates that said *Eric.*

Was it Eric Sullivan? And if so, why was he visiting Moustache Craft Ales? Slowly, my fingers reached for the ignition and silenced the engine. I watched through the window as who I assumed to be Eric parked but didn't exit his vehicle. Reaching for the binoculars again, I watched. What was he waiting for? Was he here to buy drugs too? My heart rate kicked up a notch at the thought. Galloway had been right. Firefly Bay had a drug problem.

The side door to the pub opened, but the figure that stepped out was not Jay Byrne. My eyes rounded as I watched Leah Dunn furtively glance around before making a beeline for the range rover.

With binoculars glued to my face, I barely breathed while watching the scene unfold before me. Leah didn't approach the driver's side window as Jay had done. She headed straight to the passenger door, opened it, and slid inside. Fortunately for me, Eric Sullivan did not have tinted windows. I could see everything that transpired inside the vehicle.

Dropping the binoculars into my lap, I blinked in shock. "Well. That was unexpected."

"What?" Dean asked from the passenger seat. I squeaked in fright, hand over my wildly beating heart.

"Do not do that!" I practically yelled.

"What?" he repeated.

"Suddenly appear like that, with no warning. I thought I was alone in the car."

He ignored me, his gaze traveling to the parking lot of Moustache Craft Ales. Uh oh. I tried to distract him. The last thing I needed was a ghost throwing a tantrum. "What are you doing here anyway?"

"Besides avoiding your annoying friend, the bent cop, I'm here to check in on my pub. It is, after all, my business."

"Not anymore. You're dead, remember? And Ben is not a bent cop," I snapped.

Dean leaned toward me, reached out a hand to press my shoulder into my seat so he could get a better view of the parking lot, but his hand didn't connect. It merely gave me an icy chill that I tried to scoot away from.

"Wait a minute," he hissed, eyes narrowing. "Is that…" He moved even closer, was partially submerged with the gear stick, and encroaching way too close into my personal space for any semblance of comfort. "Hot damn, it is. That son of a—"

"Hey now!" I cut in before things got ugly, and I heard words I didn't want to hear.

Dean shot across me, the road, and the lot and stood in front of the Land Rover, waving his arms and shouting like a lunatic. A totally wasted effort since I was the only one who could see or hear him. Eric and Leah remained oblivious, but then, they were engaged in a pretty epic lip lock and were essentially oblivious to everything, not just Dean.

Keeping my eye on the couple in the Land Rover and the ghost who was going ballistic, slamming his fists on the hood and kicking at the tires, or at least trying to, I felt around in my bag, searching for my phone without looking. Eventually, I retrieved it and called Galloway.

"Couple of things," I said when he answered.

He chuckled. "Hello to you too."

"Right. Sorry. Hi!" I added brightly. "So, couple of things…"

"Hit me."

"Jay Byrne is a drug dealer. I just saw him do a deal in the parking lot of Moustache Craft Ales with someone in a red hatchback."

"You're certain it was drugs?"

"Reasonably. I saw Jay hand over a baggie and then shove cash into his pocket. If not drugs, then something shady for sure."

There was silence, then I heard the clacking of the computer keyboard. "Good work." Galloway turned his attention back to me. "I'll look into it. There could be a connection between Jay and Arlie. Maybe Jay was an inside man hired to keep an eye on Dean. What else? You said there were two things?"

"Eric Sullivan and Leah Dunn are having an affair." I glanced toward the embracing couple across the street. "At least I think so."

"You think so?"

I told Galloway about the couple kissing in Eric's car. "But to be fair, maybe this is the first kiss? The first meeting? Maybe they've denied their feelings all this time because of Dean, but now that he's dead, they figure they've got nothing to lose." I finished in a rush.

"Doubtful, but a possibility, I guess."

We lapsed into silence, each lost in our own thoughts before another thought filtered through my brain. "Out of interest, do you have the autopsy report on Dean yet?"

"Not yet. Why's that?"

"I figured that'd narrow down our suspects, right? Like, it'll tell us if the killer was left or right-handed, how tall, that type of thing."

"It will assist in determining those things, for sure. I'll share what I can."

Galloway and I had an understanding. He'd share what police resources and information he was legally able to, while I shared anything I discovered in my own investigations. Galloway was hampered by things like warrants and probable cause, whereas I could access phone and financial records without such restrictions. Of course, anything I provided was not admissible in court because, you know, hacking was frowned upon. As was breaking and entering. I guess we both walked a very fine ethical line.

"What are you up to now?" Galloway asked.

"I'm going to head home and do some digging

into Leah and Eric. Financials, phone records, and such. You?"

"Bring Jay in for questioning. Arlie may not be behind Dean's death, but that's not to say one of his men didn't take matters into his own hands."

"I'll see you tonight?"

"You can bet on it."

# 8

I was rattled. It wasn't often I was rattled, and I have to say, not a fan. I blamed it on the lack of caffeine. "Did you just... pee? On the floor?"

Laura held her swollen belly and looked at her damp feet in astonishment before raising her eyes and pinning me with an incredulous look. "I think my water just broke," she said, deadpan.

I looked from her to the puddle on the floor and back again. She'd called and asked me to drop off a new mop since she was on a cleaning frenzy and the head had snapped off her current one. Since I wasn't actually getting paid to work on Dean's case, I decided it couldn't hurt to take a little time out to help my sister. I had not expected her to pee on the floor as soon as I walked in.

"You don't know?" I asked.

"This didn't happen with Isabelle. They broke her waters at the hospital."

"Right." I nodded. "So… what now?" I had zero experience with breaking waters and what it meant.

"Let me call my midwife."

"Shall I call Brad?" I felt useless in the grip of her imminent labor. Although I guess I could clean up the puddle of fluid, despite the mere thought of it making me want to gag.

"I'll do it. Once I know what's going on." She went to take a step then stopped, one hand cradling her belly, the other pressing her lower back. "Could you bring me my phone? I don't want to drip all over the floor."

*Too late.* "Sure."

She pointed to the kitchen counter.

I retrieved her phone and then got busy snapping on the rubber gloves I found abandoned in the sink and grabbing a paper towel roll.

As I mopped up, I half-listened to Laura's conversation. A lot of yes, no, oh really, okay then. I was none the wiser what the plan was.

"Aaaaarrrrggghhhhh!"

Her scream startled me so badly I fell over backward, slamming my head against an armchair. "Ow!" I complained, rubbing my head and eyeballing my sister, who was curled over, puffing and panting. "What's wrong with you?" I know, I know, it was a stupid question, and I regretted it as soon as the words had left my mouth.

"Labor." She panted. "Gotta get to the hospital."

"Now? But it only just started. Doesn't it take, like, days?"

The contraction had apparently passed, for Laura straightened and smiled at my naivety. "They want me at the hospital because my water broke. Don't worry. The baby is hours away, though hopefully not days. Toss me some of the paper towel, will you?"

I dutifully tore off half a dozen sheets and threw them at her. Wadding them up, she shoved them down her pants, a sight I never wanted to witness ever again, and waddled away, calling over her shoulder, "I'm going to take a shower and get cleaned up. Can you call Brad? Tell him he needs to come home and take me to the hospital. Oh, and call Mom? She'll need to collect Isabelle from daycare this afternoon." She sounded so calm, whereas I was on edge as anxiety crept in.

"On it." I finished cleaning up the puddle, tossed

the soggy towels, then called Brad. It went to voice mail. "Dude. Baby alert. Phone home." Then I called Mom.

"Darling, have they found out who killed that poor man on your front lawn?" Mom answered.

"Not yet."

"I hope you're staying with Kade until this is all over. It's not safe for you at home."

The thought hadn't crossed my mind. "Um. I'm not, but I'm okay. I'm safe, Mom. I keep my doors locked, and Galloway installed that alarm system a while back, remember? Anyway, Dean Ward was killed on my front lawn, not in my house." Hardly a reassuring distinction, but I ran with it.

A long heartfelt wail echoed from upstairs.

"What was that?" Mom asked sharply.

"That was Laura. She's in labor."

"At your house?" Mom asked, clearly confused.

"No, I'm at her place. She called and asked if I'd pick up a new mop for her. Quite timely, too, considering her water just broke all over the floor!"

"Oh, my!"

"Exactly." Another bellow reached my ears. I had no idea my sister had such volume. "Look, Mom, I'd better go check on her. The reason I'm calling is can you pick up Isabelle from daycare this afternoon? Obviously, Laura and Brad are going to be tied up."

"Of course. I'll let you go. Tell Laura I love her."

We hung up, and I hurried upstairs to the bathroom. The shower was running, steam rolling out into the hallway, while Laura stood under the spray, head tilted back, vocalizing her pain as contractions squeezed her body.

"Is this normal?" I asked in concern, reaching for a towel to help her out of the shower.

"What? Labor?" She grunted, allowing me to wrap the towel around her, both of us choosing to ignore the fact that she was stark naked.

"No, more… the intensity of your contractions? Your water broke five minutes ago, and now you're wailing like a banshee, and if each scream represents a contraction… Laura? They're awfully close together. Do I need to call an ambulance?"

"Don't be silly. We have hours to go. Did you get hold of Brad?"

"Left him a voice mail, but I'll try again. Lemme try from your phone. He'll pick up if he sees it's you calling."

Laura stiffened then reached for me, clenching her fingers into my shoulders until I thought for sure she'd pierced the skin. I felt powerless seeing her in such pain and had no clue what I was meant to do. Still, I remembered from countless television shows and movies that she was supposed to breathe, and judging by Laura's red face, she was currently holding her breath.

"Breathe through it," I urged, sucking in a breath through my nose and then letting it out through my mouth as if I needed to demonstrate how to breathe in case she'd forgotten. She mimicked me, and slowly, her death grip on my shoulders eased.

"Passed?" I asked, chewing my lip. There was barely a minute between contractions. Was that normal? I had no clue, but my sixth sense wasn't just tingling. It was ringing alarm bells.

"Yes. You're right. They're close. I'll get dressed, and we'll go. You can drive me. Brad will have to meet us at the hospital. In my closet is my hospital bag. Get it and put it in your car, then come back and help me down the stairs. Last thing I need is a fall mid contraction."

We were halfway to the hospital when I spied a red hatchback behind me. Was it the same one I'd seen earlier at Moustache Craft Ales? I couldn't be one hundred percent sure since Laura's wails and my inability to get a hold of Brad were severely interfering with my concentration. Not to mention I was driving one-handed as Laura had a death grip on my other hand that was threatening to break bones.

I sped into the emergency bay and skidded to a halt with a screech of tires, went to leap out to get help for Laura, only she hadn't released her grip on my hand. I nearly dislocated my shoulder as I ricocheted back toward her.

"Ow," I whimpered, knowing full well my pain was nothing in comparison to hers. "Laura, honey? Let go of my hand, sweetheart, while I go get us some help. We're at the hospital. It's all going to be okay, okay?"

She nodded, her face flushed and bathed in sweat as she puffed and panted her way through another contraction. The second she let go of my hand, I sprinted inside shouting, "Help! We need help out here. Baby imminent."

Two nurses rushed past me, while another followed with a wheelchair.

"Audrey!" I heard Laura cry and quickly returned to her side.

"It's okay. I'm here." I handed the keys to one of the nurses. "Could someone move my car? I don't think she's going to let me leave her side, and I haven't been able to reach her husband."

The next hour was a blur. Laura was whisked up to delivery, and like it or not, I was her unprepared birthing partner. I took her phone and called Brad while the nurses settled Laura and took her vitals. Again, straight to voice mail. "Brad, we're at the hospital, and your child is intent on making a speedy delivery into the world. You need to be here. Now!"

After hanging up, I chewed my lip, wondering what could be keeping him. On the off chance he was in a meeting and didn't have his phone with him, I rang his office and left a message with the receptionist, who, after my frantic call, immediately went to hunt him down in person. I was confident he'd arrive in time for the birth of his child.

I was wrong. Laura's labor was the most intense experience of my life. After witnessing it firsthand, I wasn't sure I ever wanted kids. Her screams were gut-wrenching. I'd never heard my sister so vocal before and nor had my eardrums, but her pain had me feeling utterly helpless and useless. She was sucking on the gas like her life depended on it, begging for an epidural, but the midwife said it was too late, baby was almost here, then, with a final almighty push, the baby arrived. There was lots of fluid and blood, and the entire thing looked like a crime scene.

The delivery room was eerily silent for three seconds, then a small cry pierced the silence. Baby Nicholson had arrived.

"Congratulations, it's a girl!" The midwife beamed and placed a squirming little body covered in… something I couldn't identify on Laura's chest.

"You did it!" I beamed, my eyes inexplicably filling with tears. I'd stayed by Laura's side the entire time, not wanting to go down near the business end of things and accidentally catch a glimpse of my sister's hoohaa. I love her dearly, but there are limits.

Cuddling her newborn, Laura smiled up at me, and it was all there in her face. The love, the utter devotion to this tiny human she'd created. "Thanks for staying."

"You're welcome, but I don't really think I had a choice. Your grip was incredible. You been working out?"

We both giggled at the very idea. "I wonder where my husband is?" Laura glanced at the door as if expecting Brad to come busting through. He didn't.

"I rang him from my phone and yours. And I called his office. The receptionist is looking for him. He can't be far off."

"He'll be so upset he missed the birth."

"Baby Nicholson sure was in a hurry to arrive. I was worried you were going to pop her out on my front seat."

"Can you imagine?" Laura snorted.

"The stain? Yes, yes, I can."

Laura chuckled and slapped at my arm. "Thank you, though. Seriously."

I leaned down and wrapped her and the baby in a warm embrace. "Congratulations again. She's utterly perfect. Do you have a name for her?"

Laura laid her head back with a weary smile. "We do, but I'll wait until Brad gets here."

"Fair enough."

Brad arrived ten minutes later, tie pulled loose, the top buttons of his shirt undone. Yep, the harried look of an expectant father. I was about to slip out to give the new family some alone time when Laura stopped me.

With one arm cradling her baby and the other hand clasped in her husband's, she beamed. "Audrey? We'd like you to meet your niece, Grace Elizabeth."

I gently stroked Grace's cheek with the back of my finger. "Welcome to the world Grace Elizabeth. I'm your Aunt Audrey. You'll soon learn I'm the fun one," I added on a whisper. Laura snorted, and Brad chuckled.

"Okay, guys, I'm gonna head off, leave you all to get acquainted with your daughter. I'll come back later for another visit, though."

Brad pulled me in for a hug, squashing me against his side so tight I could barely breathe. "Thank you for taking care of them."

"Anytime." I wheezed, not meaning it. Birth appeared to be horrendously painful and a one hundred percent messy affair. My yearning for children of my own plummeted considerably after witnessing Grace's arrival into the world, and coupling that with my worry that my clumsiness would endanger a child if I were to ever have one, I was starting to think babies of my own were not in my future.

I was mulling over that worrying thought as I drove away. Security had taken care of my car, and when I'd returned to the emergency department, they'd been kind enough to retrieve it for me, valet style. Still, now it was time to get back to the business of finding out who killed Dean Ward. I'd worry about babies, or the lack thereof, later.

# 9

My background searches on Eric Sullivan and Leah Dunn failed to turn up anything useful. No sudden influx or expenditure of large sums of money. No calls to or from the pay-as-you-go number I'd pulled from Dean's records. But what I did have were numerous text messages between Leah and Eric, dating back three months. While I could see they'd messaged each other, I couldn't see what those messages said. I could only assume they were arranging to meet up to carry out their illicit affair, but there was only one way to know for sure. Ask them.

"You coming?" I asked Ben, who'd been hovering over my shoulder all afternoon.

"Of course. I may be able to use my ghostly juju and read the messages on Eric's phone."

"How do you know I'm going to see Eric first? Maybe I'm going to see Leah."

"Because you don't like Leah. She's your last resort. Therefore it makes sense that you'll go see Eric first, and I'm confident that between the two of us, we can get to the truth."

I screwed up my nose. He was right, of course. I didn't like Leah, and I didn't particularly want to go and see her. Not yet anyway. Not when I didn't have all the answers.

"Have you seen Dean around?" I asked, gathering up my things.

"Nope. Don't want to, either."

"What is it with you two?"

Ben shrugged. "You heard him. He was one of the ones to jump on the bent cop train when I left the force. Was pretty vocal about it too. Probably because I'd arrested him once."

"Dean has a record?" Why hadn't anyone mentioned this before now? This could change everything.

"He spent a night in the cells to sober up. Drunk and disorderly. No conviction recorded, so no criminal record," Ben explained.

"Damn."

"My thoughts exactly." Ben followed me out to the car and was already seated in the passenger seat by the time I opened the driver's side door. It still gave me the heebie-jeebies watching him walk through solid objects, but I had to admit, it was a pretty cool skill to have. The downside was he couldn't touch anything, not physically.

Turning into Firefly Bay Brewing Company's parking lot a few minutes later, I was surprised to see a familiar red hatchback. "See that car?" I pointed to it.

"Yeah. What about it?" Ben asked.

"I need to know who owns it. Can you take a look, see if there's anything inside that'd help identify the owner?"

"On it."

I left Ben poking around in the hatchback while I made my way into the pub. It was late afternoon, the lull between lunch and dinner, with few patrons in attendance.

"What can I get you?" The bartender, a blonde woman in her forties with a hot pink streak in her hair, paused in wiping down the bar.

"I need a word with the boss. Eric."

She wiped her hands on a towel and walked away

without a word. Presumably to let Eric know I was here, but who knows, maybe she was miffed I hadn't ordered a drink.

"Miss Fitzgerald, what can I do for you?" Eric approached barely a minute later, a welcoming smile on his face, but I didn't miss the hint of wariness in his eyes.

"Please, call me Audrey." I offered my own smile, knowing it didn't reach my eyes and not caring in the least. "Is there somewhere we can talk?"

"Here's fine."

I raised a brow. Well, tried to. Both of them shot upward. "You sure?"

"There's nothing you can say to me that can't be said here." He postured, and I almost laughed.

"Okay then. How long have you been having an affair with Leah Dunn?" I asked.

The bartender paused in drying a glass to blatantly listen in.

"And no point denying it. I saw the two of you myself, pashing in the parking lot of Moustache Craft Ales."

A wave of red washed over Eric's face, and he snapped a look at the bartender, who quickly returned to drying her already dry glass. "Let's take this to my office," he grumbled.

"Hey," I threw my hands in the air and followed him, "I did offer that in the first place, but you wanted to talk at the bar."

"All right, all right, I get your point."

His office was tiny and cramped. There was one desk shoved against the wall, a chair, and two filing cabinets. He leaned back against his desk and nodded toward the door.

"Shut that, will you?"

"So, you do care about people overhearing?" I shut the door. There was nowhere to sit, so I leaned back against the door and did my best not to look awkward. Thank goodness I wasn't claustrophobic because the office had no window, and with the door closed, I could practically feel the walls closing in. Maybe I was a little claustrophobic after all.

Eric didn't answer, just crossed his arms over his chest and asked, "What do you want?"

"I want to know how long you and Leah have been having an affair. And where were you the night Dean died?"

"You think I killed him? That's ridiculous!" he blustered.

"Just answer the questions."

"Okay, fine! Just over three months. Leah and I have been seeing each other for just over three months, and I couldn't have killed Dean because I was with her that night. Or rather, she was with me."

"Where?"

"At my house."

"Can anyone collaborate that? Did anyone see her?"

"The whole idea of keeping a relationship secret is that no-one sees you."

Fair point. "What about your daughter? Does she live at home?"

"She does, but we're careful her and Leah don't cross paths. Megan is twenty. She's out most of the time anyway, and when she does come home, it's usually the early hours of the morning. Leah never sleeps over. She's gone by then."

"Must be harrowing, though, hoping the two of them don't bump into each other coming and going."

"We're careful."

"Not today, though. You were in a rather heated embrace in public view in the middle of the day."

"We were in my car." Eric protested. "No one was around."

"I was."

"I hardly think a PI catching us counts. No doubt you had surveillance equipment."

Damn. Got me.

He uncrossed his arms, placed them on his hips, and met my look head-on. "Look, I don't deny I'm in love with Leah and have been since I first laid eyes on her. Yes, I was hurt and angry when Dean stole her from me. Yes, it ruined both our friendship and our business arrangement, but I have no regrets over that. I've done okay without him. He and Leah weren't married. In fact, he'd told her he had no intention of ever getting married or having children."

"And that's something Leah wanted?" I guessed.

"Doesn't every woman?"

I don't know. Do they? I thought I did, but after today, I was starting to have reservations. But that had nothing to do with Eric, so I kept my mouth shut.

"How did the affair start?" I asked instead.

"Leah approached me for some advice regarding their application for the Craft Ale of the Year award."

I snorted. "What? And you helped her?"

He shook his head. "Of course not. Why would I? I wanted that award for myself."

"And you got it."

"I did. But we got to talking, and it sounds cliché, but one thing led to another."

"And what were your plans? Where did the two

of you see this going? Was she going to leave Dean? After all, you just said he had no intention of marrying her or having children. I'm guessing that's something you were prepared to offer?"

"She was waiting for the right time. She was worried about him. Said he hadn't been himself. She thought he may be depressed and might do something stupid if she left him."

"Did she stop to think he wasn't himself and was depressed because he knew about the affair?" I knew that wasn't the case. Dean had been furious when he'd caught them today. His reaction was one of utter surprise. Dean hadn't known Leah was cheating on him, but that didn't mean he hadn't suspected something. Maybe that was why he wanted to hire me?

Eric was silent for a moment then blurted, "It was business-related. She's going to be mad I told you, but heck, it's probably going to come out sooner or later. Moustache Craft Ales was in serious financial trouble and was going under. I'd say in a matter of weeks."

"I know. I'm a PI, remember?"

Eric barked out a laugh. "Of course."

"So she was waiting until he lost his business and

then was going to leave him?" Talk about kicking a man when he's down.

"No. She was going to see him through it. Wait until he got back on his feet first."

I blinked. "That could be a hell of a long wait. One doesn't simply bounce back from bankruptcy."

Eric rolled a shoulder in a shrug. Did he think the same thing, that Leah could potentially tie herself to Dean for years before eventually leaving him? Maybe Eric decided the quickest way to deal with Dean was to kill him, then he could have Leah all to himself.

Changing tack, I asked, "So, Leah was with you the night Dean died. What time did she leave?"

"I was half asleep, but I heard the stairs creak around one a.m. and figured it was her leaving."

I didn't have Dean's exact time of death, but I did know it was after midnight. I made a mental note to ask Galloway to see if Leah's alibi lined up. Reaching behind me, I twisted the door handle. "Thanks for your time." Eric didn't reply, but I felt his gaze boring into my back as I walked away.

I paused before leaving the pub, my eyes scanning the patrons. Someone here owned that red hatchback. There was a couple in their fifties, three guys wearing reflective shirts and construction gear having an early lunch, two men who looked mid-twenties playing pool, and a group of eight women rowdily declaring *book club* open. I focused on them and sidled closer to eavesdrop. They were of the soccer mom variety, no talk of books but plenty of their respective kids and husbands. Was one of them popping pills to help her get through the day?

But none of them looked like they'd be driving the red hatchback either. It was an older car, a little beaten up, a little faded. And there was no child's seat in the back.

Ben hadn't turned up yet, so I went out to the lot to find him still rummaging through the car.

"How's it going?" I asked, standing next to the car and talking on my phone as if taking a call.

"This car is a rubbish dump on wheels," he complained, dusting his hands on his thighs. I cast a quick glance inside. He was right. Burger wrappers and take-out cups covered the floor in the back.

"Doubtful this car belongs to a parent." I sighed.

"A parent? Nah, this is a young person's car. Female."

"Female?"

"Yeah, makeup all over the passenger seat, like she does her makeup while she drives. How did it go with Eric?"

"He admitted to the affair. He says Leah was with him the night of the murder, that he heard her leaving around one in the morning."

"And all Dean remembers is that it was after midnight when he came to see you."

"She told Eric she was going to leave Dean but was waiting until he'd gotten through his financial crisis. She said he seemed depressed and was worried he'd do something silly."

"What? Like, kill himself? Dean Ward is the last person I'd call suicidal."

"He was about to go bankrupt," I pointed out. "That can be humiliating."

Ben shrugged. "He's not the first, won't be the last. In fact..." He paused, lost in thought, before snapping his fingers soundlessly. "In fact, that could have been a genius move on his behalf."

"Genius? How?"

"He's up to his neck in shady dealings with Arlie Roberts, right? According to him, he wanted out, but Arlie had him over a barrel. What better way to get that particular monkey off your back than by declaring bankruptcy?"

"But he'd lose Moustache Craft Ales. The business he was desperately trying to protect." It didn't seem like a winning strategy to me. Sure, it would get him out of the deal he'd made with Arlie Roberts because there'd be no more pub. But also, there'd be no more pub.

"He was trying to protect his liquor license," Ben said. "We need to go look at how he set things up, but my guess is the liquor license is attached to his name, not the business itself."

"Meaning?"

"Meaning if Moustache Craft Ales were to declare bankruptcy, the liquor license might not be considered an asset."

"So, it couldn't be sold with the business to recoup losses and pay creditors." I nodded. Now it made sense.

"Exactly. But I could be wrong. We need to see who owns the license and who owns the business and who is liable when it comes to bankruptcy."

"Let's go." I headed toward my own car, Ben beating me to it.

"What about the hatchback?" He jerked his thumb in the direction of the red car.

"Shoot. I should get a shot of the plate. Hang on." I leaped out of the car, dashed into the middle of the parking lot, and snapped a quick picture of the rear of the hatch, including the plate.

Back in the car, Ben turned to me. "You do know

there are probably dozens of red hatchbacks in Firefly Bay and that you don't know for sure that this is the one you saw earlier."

"You're right. I don't. It's a long shot."

"So, what's the plan? Take a photo of every red hatch that you see and run the plate?"

My mouth turned down at the corners. "I know it's a scattergun approach, but I know what I saw, and that person bought drugs from Jay Byrne."

"Your efforts would be better spent investigating him. Getting a dealer off the streets trumps persecuting a buyer."

I paused. He was right. I was so focused on who the red hatchback driver was when in reality, I should be focused on Jay. Who was his supplier? Where was he getting the drugs from?

"Watching you think is both hilarious and painful." Ben chuckled. "Let me help you out. First things first, let's focus on who killed Dean Ward. I'll be much happier when his ghost isn't hanging around. Then go after Jay."

"You're right. They may even be connected. Two birds, one stone." Just as the words left my mouth, the three spirits I'd seen last time I'd been at Firefly Bay Brewing Company drifted through the front wall of the pub. Like before, they hovered in the air, dark mist rolling around and beneath them. They were almost shapeless, yet I could just make out the silhouette of a man. Well, three men.

"Can you see them?" I whispered to Ben, barely moving, barely able to breathe. The air was heavy, and a feeling of dread invaded my bones. I didn't like these spirits, didn't like the way they made me feel.

"Holy sh—" he gasped, eyes as wide as saucers. "Who the heck are they?"

"Don't know. I saw them last time I was here too."

"Are you going to… you know… talk to them?"

I started the car and bolted out of the parking lot. "No," I gritted through my teeth. Call me a chicken, but those spirits scared me.

# 10

Leah Dunn wasn't home. No surprises there—it was coming into the busiest time of the day for a pub, and I assumed she was at Moustache Craft Ales. I wondered what would happen to the place now that Dean was dead. His debts still needed to be paid off. Leah's bank account wasn't exactly flush, so there was no way she could afford to buy the place. Would Eric step in, snap it up as an investment?

"Keep a lookout," I instructed Ben, crouching in front of Leah's door and sliding a pick into the lock from my lock picking kit.

"What y'all doing?" Dean appeared directly in front of me, half in half out of the door.

"Aaah!" I fell onto my rear, heart thundering in my chest, the pick falling to the ground.

"Oh. This is one of those *don't do that* moments, isn't it?" Dean surmised. "Sorry if I startled you." His words might have said he was sorry, but his tone conveyed otherwise. Ignoring him, I scooped up the pick and repositioned myself.

"You're picking the lock?" Dean stood to the side with arms crossed over his chest. "Let me save you some trouble. There's a spare key beneath that plant pot."

Heavens to Betsy. Dropping my chin to my chest, I sucked in a deep, calming breath. Why hadn't I thought to search for a spare key in the first place? And why was Dean being helpful?

"Thanks," I grunted, putting the pick away and shoving the kit into my back pocket. Lifting the bright yellow potted plant Dean had pointed to, I retrieved the key.

"Is there anything in here you think we should know about?" I asked him as I unlocked the door and stepped inside.

"I've got nothing to hide."

I snorted. "You've been hiding plenty. Illegal booze, about to go bankrupt," I ticked off on my fingers. "You haven't been exactly forthcoming. Did you know Leah was having an affair? With Eric?" His reaction earlier seemed genuine. Their affair was news to him, but then Dean was so full of ego and himself that I doubt he'd admit they'd successfully fooled him.

The air crackled, and Dean's visage took on a red hue.

"I'd say that's a no," Ben stage whispered from the corner of his mouth.

"Agreed." I pulled out a pair of latex gloves from my pocket and snapped them on, belatedly remembering to give the door handle a wipe with the hem of my T-shirt before heading toward the bookcase in the living room.

"I can do that," Ben interrupted me. Holding out his hand, fingers splayed, he ran them through the books.

"I thought you couldn't feel anything?" I said. "What's that going to prove, other than that you can wave your hand through a bunch of books?"

"I can't feel them physically. But I can feel their… energy, for want of a better word. It's hard to describe, but I can feel when something is out of place."

"You're saying you can feel if something is hidden in one of those books?"

He nodded. "Try this one. Something is in the pages."

I pulled down the book in question and flipped through the pages. A quarter of the way through was a bookmark. "Nice try." I put the book back.

"Can't win 'em all. But I'll keep going here. Why don't you go search the bedroom?"

I did, pulling out drawers, feeling for fake backs or bottoms. Nothing.

"What exactly are you looking for?" Dean asked, watching me.

I shrugged. "Anything out of place. Anything you or Leah have hidden that may help with finding out who killed you."

"I need to ask you something." Dean's voice was low and furtive, and I paused in looking under the bed to glance at him.

"What?"

"This ghost business. How does it work? Exactly."

"Um. I'm not sure I know what you mean. All I know is that sometimes when someone dies unexpectedly or violently, their ghost remains behind."

He nodded. "And you can see them."

"Yes."

"Why's that?"

"We think it's due to someone trying to cast a

healing spell when Ben was killed. It somehow connected his spirit to me, giving me this ability."

"And what happens after?"

"After?"

"After you find out who killed me? Do I stay, or do I go? I'm assuming that's what this is all about—unfinished business and all that. And if I go, where do I go?"

"This hasn't happened a whole lot, but usually, when a murder is solved, the ghost moves on. Where they go, I have no idea. Heaven? Hell? Some other afterlife?"

"But Delaney's murder was solved. I remember reading about it in the paper. And he's still here."

"By choice." I nodded.

"And the other ghosts?"

"What other ghosts?"

"The three old creepy men."

I froze. "Are you talking about the three spirits that float off the ground accompanied by a black fog?"

"Yeah, those guys. What's their deal?"

"I don't know. The first time I saw them was at Firefly Bay Brewing Company."

"I think they're after me." I didn't miss the note of

fear tinging Dean's words, and I can't say I blamed him. The spirits rattled me too.

"What makes you say that?"

"Because they keep turning up wherever I go."

"Have you spoken with them?"

"No way! I hightail it out of there."

"So, you just keep running away?" Not that I could blame him I'd done the same thing.

He nodded. "They don't move fast. And one of the cool things about this ghost business is I can disappear and reappear anywhere I want. So, I just bounce whenever they show up."

I resumed searching under the bed. "Interesting." I had no answer for Dean about who the three spirits were and why they were following him, other than they were creepy, and I got a very distinct bad vibe from their presence, which basically meant, if they did finally catch up with him, it wouldn't be good.

"Hello," I muttered to myself, stretching to pick up what appeared to be a cufflink. "Yours?" I held it up to the light, only as I twisted it, I saw the initials ES. Oops. Not Dean's. Eric's. So he'd lied when he said they always hooked up at his house. Why else would his cufflink be underneath Leah's bed?

"That low-down piece of—" Dean cursed, fingers

clenching into fists. "I'm gonna make him pay!" Then, he promptly disappeared.

"Ben!" I called out.

"What's up?" He appeared in the bedroom doorway, crossing to examine the cufflink I still held between my fingers. "Guess that belongs to Eric, huh?"

"I'd say so. Dean is off on another tantrum; he's gone after Eric. Can you go and keep an eye on him? I don't think he can actually inflict any damage, but you never know. A ghost on a rampage may be able to do more harm than we realize."

"On it."

I spent another hour searching Leah's apartment, finding nothing more of interest. Standing in the kitchen staring at the photo of Eric, Leah, and Dean pinned to the fridge, I remembered my first visit here. Leah had been pretty emphatic that Eric was responsible for Dean's death. It struck me as odd that she'd throw him under the bus like that, considering she was sleeping with him and apparently making plans to leave Dean. Although that part was somewhat murky.

"This case is the pits," I muttered, letting myself out and placing the key back under the yellow pot. Snapping off the latex gloves, I tossed them on the passenger seat and then sat with the engine running while mulling over my next move. "I keep going around in circles. Dean was a whisker away from bankruptcy. He was in over his head with Arlie Roberts. Yet Galloway doesn't think Arlie is responsible for Dean's murder. He has a point. Arlie would be cutting off an income stream by killing Dean. Then we have Leah's affair with Eric. Her behavior is beyond strange—her almost hysterical grief at Dean's death then accusing Eric of Dean's murder despite having an affair with Eric. It just doesn't add up."

I wriggled the cufflink out of my pocket and looked at it. Tossing it in the air, I closed my fist to catch it, only I missed, and it fell to the floor of the car. I spent the next five minutes searching for it. Once I'd retrieved it and stashed it back in my pocket, I decided on my next course of action. Search Eric's house.

Ten minutes later, I was parked three doors down from Eric Sullivan's place. Grabbing the latex gloves I'd discarded earlier, I walked along the sidewalk, eyeing the neighbors' houses. Everything was quiet, no one was about as I turned up Eric's driveway. No cars. I hoped that meant both he and his daughter were out.

Sidling around to the rear of the house, I crouched by the back door, retrieved the leather pouch I kept my lock picking tools in from my back pocket, and proceeded to pick the lock. I was in within seconds. I'd excelled at this task during my training. Galloway had said it was uncanny how quickly I'd taken to getting into anything locked. It seemed only fair that I was good at something since I'd yet to master the art of gunmanship.

Once inside, I stood for a moment to get not only my bearings but the house's general layout. Then I froze. Was that a phone ringing? Someone was home after all! I backtracked faster than a hot knife through butter, only to my utter confusion, once I was outside, the ringing was louder. And it was coming from the garbage can at the corner of the house.

Glancing around as if I was about to be punked, I cautiously made my way to the garbage can and lifted the lid. Inside, a cell phone vibrated, its ring-tone echoing loudly. A half second's debate with myself on whether I should answer or not was quickly decided.

Careful not to touch the phone to my face, I answered, "Hello?"

"Who's this?" a male voice demanded. A very familiar male voice.

I frowned. "Galloway?"

A second's hesitation, then, "Audrey?"

"Yeah. It's me."

"What are you doing with that phone?"

"Uh. Yeah." I bit my lip sheepishly. "So, I'm at Eric's house…"

"Eric Sullivan's?"

"Yep."

"It's his phone?"

"Well, now, that I couldn't say. It was in the garbage can out back. I heard it ringing. Thought it really odd that a garbage can was ringing. Why throw out a perfectly good phone?"

"Maybe because it's the phone that belongs to that pay-as-you-go number Dean Ward called before he died," Galloway said, deadpan.

"Oh." I held the phone away and squinted at it before putting it back to my ear. All without touching because a) evidence and b) germs. It had been in the garbage, after all. "Do you want me to bring it in?"

"I want you to stay where you are. Do not move. I'll send someone to you. We need to preserve the evidence and chain of custody."

Whatever that meant. "Okay. Bye," I said brightly and hung up. Then, unsure what I was supposed to do with the phone, I decided to put it back where I found it. Then I settled in to wait while silently praying neither Eric nor his daughter would return home and discover me loitering in their back garden.

Color me surprised when Galloway himself turned up. He'd said he was sending someone, so I was expecting a uniform, not *Captain Cowboy Hot Pants* himself. Not that I was complaining, mind you. He was always a sight for sore eyes.

"You have something you want to tell me?" he asked, arms crossed.

I hunched my shoulders and tried not to look guilty. "No. Why?"

"You sure?" he pressed. Surely, he wasn't waiting for me to confess that I'd let myself into Eric's house? I'd only been in there a minute before the phone had rung, leading me back outside.

"The phone's in there." I pointed to the garbage can. He glanced at it and back at me. I frowned, not sure what he was waiting for, what he wanted me to say.

"What?" I finally snapped, starting to get annoyed.

He sighed and shook his head. "Does your sister ring any bells? Something about a baby?"

"Oh! Right!" I slapped my forehead. "Sorry, yes." I plastered a smile on my face. "Laura had her baby. A girl. Grace Elizabeth."

"So I heard."

"Are you mad you didn't hear it from me?" I blinked in shock. I admit, it was poor form of me not to let him know, but I didn't think he'd be mad about it. Truth be told, I was still digesting the trauma. When I'd gotten up that morning, I hadn't been expecting to witness the birth of a baby. And I definitely hadn't been expecting that event to change my stance on having my own babies, yet here we were.

He shook his head and sighed. "I'm not mad at you, Audrey. I'm concerned."

"You are?"

"Yes."

"Why?"

"Because Laura called and said you left the hospital shell shocked, and she realized that maybe being there for the birth of Grace was a little… overwhelming."

I was silent for a moment, trying not to twitch. I did not want to talk about this. Not now. Maybe never. I was very good at avoidance.

I pointed to the garbage can. "Did I tell you the phone's in there?"

"Fine." He shook open an evidence bag and retrieved the phone, dropping it into the bag. "We'll talk about this later."

"The phone?"

"The baby."

Oh, goody. I could hardly wait.

"Do I want to know what you're doing here?" He nodded toward the house.

I shook my head. "You do not."

His gray eyes narrowed, and he looked at me so intently my mouth dried, and I could barely swallow. He took two long strides toward me with another shake of his head and swept me into his arms, cradling me close to his chest.

"You drive me crazy." His voice rumbled against my ear, along with the beating of his heart. I wrapped my arms around his waist and squeezed.

"Is that a bad thing?" I whispered. I knew I'd been hard work this last week. The caffeine withdrawals had been horrendous, my mood sour. Even I didn't want to hang out with me.

"Crazy in a good way," he clarified.

"Oh, phew." I sagged against him in relief. "That's good then."

With a chuckle, he set me away from him and dropped a kiss on my mouth. "To be continued."

My favorite words. "Most definitely."

My eyes were glued to his denim encased rear, admiring the view as he walked away when he called out without turning around. "You'd better not be thinking about letting yourself into that house, Fitzgerald."

I gasped in mock outrage. "Moi? Never!" Darn it. With my sleuthing exploits temporarily foiled, I slowly followed him down the driveway, my mind awhirl.

## 11

Sometimes a girl just has to man up and do what needs to be done. Carrying a bouquet of flowers the size of a small child, I returned to the hospital to visit Laura and baby Grace. Not that seeing my sister and brand-new niece was a hardship, rather I was still having flashbacks of the birth and, quite frankly, the gore of it.

"You called Galloway." I greeted Laura with a kiss on the cheek before laying the flowers on the trolley at the foot of her bed.

"I did," she admitted freely.

"Why?"

"Come sit." She patted the side of the bed. I peeked in at Grace in her crib then eased myself onto the edge of the bed. "Audrey, you didn't see your face. You did and said all the right things, but girl, there was not a lick of color in your cheeks, and you had a totally freaked-out look of terror in your eyes. As soon as Brad turned up, you couldn't get out of here quick enough."

And here I was thinking I was being thoughtful and giving them time alone with their new family member. I pursed my lips then blew out a breath. "Okay, fine, that's true. I guess I wasn't prepared for it."

Laura held my hand. "Of course not. None of us were. What you witnessed today was a very fast labor. An hour and a half from start to finish. That isn't typical. I get that it was probably frightening. And you had no time to prepare yourself mentally."

Very true. I had limited knowledge of childbirth. Obviously, I understand the workings of where babies come from, I'm not that naive, but if I'd ever expected to be a birthing partner. I'd have put in some groundwork, watched some videos, read some books, joined Laura at birthing classes. But I was *never* expecting to be someone's birthing partner. Ever. So, I'd done none of those things.

"But why call Galloway?" I wailed because now it was on his radar, and I knew at some point I was going to have to talk to him about this whole baby thing, and I simply wasn't ready for it. Even now, chatting with Laura, my mind hadn't been changed. I was not sure I wanted children. And I just knew if those words left my lips, my family would begin a campaign to change my mind. And who knows, maybe it would work, but it was entirely unfair having to deal with it while on a caffeine fast.

"Because I was worried about you, and I couldn't be there to make sure you were okay. But he could be."

Typical of my family. Their hearts are always in the right place, but their actions often messed things up for me.

Laura frowned. "Are you upset that I called him?"

I half shrugged. "I just wished you hadn't."

"Why?" she asked, astonished. "Is everything okay with you two?"

Gah, this was going from bad to worse. Rather than answer, I turned my attention to the baby. "Is she awake? Can I hold her?"

Laura immediately turned to mush. "Of course. She's just the most adorable baby. Aside from Isabelle, of course."

I grinned. "Of course." Scooping the little bundle into my arms, I cuddled my new niece to my chest. It wasn't that I didn't like children, far from it. I loved my nieces and nephew to bits. But the birth. The pain. The blood. Did I mention the pain? Would my biological clock be appeased by lavishing my siblings' children with love rather than producing my own? Right now, the answer was a resounding yes!

I was swaying, whispering nonsense to the baby sleeping in my arms, when my brother Dustin and sister-in-law, Amanda, arrived to visit. Amanda made a beeline for me and the bundle I was holding. I dutifully handed her over.

"Missed your call this morning," I said, watching as Amanda fell in love with Grace. How could you not?

She glanced at me. "Figured you had plenty going on with your front garden a crime scene. You really should have told me that yesterday, and we could have moved the baby shower somewhere else."

"It was fine." I protested. "Only the front lawn was affected, and it's not like we were out there using it."

"Still, I wasn't expecting to arrive to find crime scene tape strewn around. I assume you're still caffeine-free? Or has this been the final straw, and you've fallen off the wagon?"

I bristled. "No falling here. I'm one hundred

percent caffeine-free. Until tomorrow." One more day.

"And how are you finding things? Any less clumsy? No longer bumping into things? More clarity and focus?"

"I'm still me if that's what you're asking," I snapped, irritation rising. My fuse was a whole lot shorter, thanks to Amanda's dare.

Dustin interrupted, demanding his turn with baby Grace. Deciding I'd had enough of Laura's loving interference and Amanda's interrogation, I bid a hasty farewell and fled for the second time. I was passing emergency when an ambulance arrived, and pure curiosity had me halting to see who they were bringing in.

"What do we have?" a nurse asked while my two favorite paramedics, Ned and Jayce, wheeled in their patient.

"Amy Baker, twenty-year-old female, suspected drug overdose."

Following behind, looking frantic and distraught, was Megan Sullivan, Eric's daughter. "Please tell me she'll be okay," she pleaded.

"What did she take?" the nurse asked.

"Unknown but suspected opioid overdose," Ned replied then rattled off a stream of stats.

Another nurse joined them, leading Megan away from her friend. "Do you know what she took? Where she got the drugs?"

"I don't know." Megan sniffed, wiping her fingers under her eyes. "We were hanging out, and she just slumped over, and I couldn't wake her up."

A doctor wearing scrubs arrived. "What do we have?"

"Unknown quantity of suspected opioids," the nurse told him. "Breath sounds are good."

The doctor listened to Amy's chest, nodding. "Keep her on the oxygen, and let's start her on activated charcoal. If her breathing slows or becomes shallow, we'll try naloxone."

They drew the curtains around Amy's treatment bay, blocking the view. Megan stood alone in the middle of the emergency department, and I approached, placing a comforting hand on her shoulder.

"I'm so sorry about your friend," I said. "But she's in good hands."

"What are you doing here?" She looked at me in surprise, not having noticed me earlier. "You're that PI lady Dad was telling me about."

"My sister just had a baby. I was visiting."

"I hope she'll be okay." Megan wrung her hands,

and I followed her gaze to the cubicle where they were working on Amy.

"Do you think she… overdosed… intentionally?"

"What?" Megan looked shaken. "No way." But then, she muttered under her breath, "I hope not."

One of the nurses returned, asking for Megan to assist with some paperwork and contact information for Amy's family. I left, deep in thought. Was it Amy I saw buying drugs from Jay?

My phone dinged, announcing a text message. Glancing at the screen, I saw it was from Galloway. Checking up on me? A sliver of discomfort danced up my spine. I really wished Laura hadn't called him. Now he was going to smother me with concern and think I was all fragile. Annoyed, I swiped open the message, already formulating a witty reply in response when I stopped and blinked. His message wasn't what I was expecting.

*Eric at station for questioning. Want to sit in?*

Does a bear poop in the woods? Heck, yeah!

*I'm on my way.* I wrote back, adding a smiley face emoji.

Jumping in my car, all thoughts of babies and births were forgotten. I drove to the station as quickly as legally possible. It wasn't often Galloway officially invited me. Usually, I just followed him in and hung around, shooting the breeze with whoever was on duty.

"Hey, Audrey, back again?" Officer Walsh grinned and slapped me on the back. "I'll let Galloway know you're here."

I eyed the coffeepot longingly. Despite knowing the brew had been sitting there all day and was probably bitter enough to strip the enamel off my teeth, I still had a mean hankering for a cup of it.

"You made good time," Galloway said, mouth close to my ear.

I swung around, a smile on my face, excited at the turn of events.

"Hospital isn't far from here. So, how does this work? Do I get to ask him questions?"

Galloway chuckled. "Hold your horses, Columbo. When I said sit in, I didn't mean sit in sit in."

I got it. He couldn't very well have a civilian sitting in on an official police interview. "You meant sit out? Behind a two-way mirror?"

"Almost." Placing a hand between my shoulder blades, Galloway led me toward the corridor running the length of the building. "You can watch—and listen—on a monitor. We record everything."

Three doors on one side of the corridor, four on the other. I already knew Galloway's office was the first door, and directly opposite was the interrogation room. He indicated the room next to that, and I preceded him inside. Not so much a room as a closet. A tiny strip of a window at the top let in a small amount of daylight. One desk was pushed up against the wall and on it sat a computer with a large monitor, keyboard, and set of headphones.

While the room itself was dark and a little dingy, the computer system was top-notch. "Nice." I nodded in approval, pulling out the chair and making myself comfortable.

"Glad you like it." Galloway leaned over my shoulder to type something, and while I was distracted with the scent of his cologne, an image appeared on the monitor. Eric Sullivan in the interview room next door.

"This computer isn't networked with the rest of the station," Galloway explained. "It has its own secure server."

"In case you get hacked." Smart. Not that I'd hack the police department, but phone records and bank statements were fair play in my line of work. I paused for a moment, wondering when it was, exactly, that I'd decided that was okay. Once upon a time, I would have balked at the very thought of it.

"Earth to Audrey." Galloway stroked a finger

down my cheek, and I leaned toward him, almost toppling off the chair.

"Everything okay?" he asked with just the right amount of concern, one hand on my shoulder to steady me.

"I'm fine." I smiled. A genuine smile, not just baring my teeth. I appreciated him not pushing me to discuss Laura and the birth of Grace.

"Right. I'm going in. I'll control the recording from in there, so don't touch anything. Just watch and listen, okay?"

Clasping my hands together, I rested them on the desktop. "No touching. Got it."

I turned my attention back to the monitor and watched Eric nervously rub one thumb with the other. He jerked when the door opened, and Galloway stepped into the room.

Galloway pulled out the chair opposite and sat, rattling off the usual date and time before asking Eric to confirm his identity.

"Yes, I'm Eric Sullivan," he confirmed.

"And do you know why you're here today, Eric?"

Eric's brows shot up. "Actually, no. I mean, I assume it has something to do with Dean's death, but I wasn't involved in that, so no, I don't know why I'm here." There was a certain tone of belligerence in his words.

Galloway placed a plastic evidence bag on the table. I recognized the phone I'd found in the garbage can at the back of Eric's house.

"Do you recognize this phone?" Galloway asked.

Eric peered at it then shook his head. "No. Should I?"

"It was found at your house."

Eric blinked, gathering his thoughts. "I sure hope you had a search warrant, Detective."

Galloway smiled. "I did. As a matter of fact, our officers are still at your house now. Are they going to find anything else?"

"What do you mean, anything else? That's a phone. Dean was stabbed. I don't see how the two are related."

"Why do you have two phones, Eric?" Galloway asked.

"I don't," he protested. He looked at the phone again. "Maybe it's—" He shut his mouth with a snap.

"Maybe it's Leah's," I whispered to myself. That's what he'd been about to say. And then he'd realized he was going to implicate the woman he loved, and he'd clammed up.

"I don't know whose phone that is, but it isn't mine." He crossed his arms and sat back in his chair.

"What about this?" Galloway laid another plastic evidence bag on the table, this one much smaller. Eric leaned forward to peer at the contents.

"It's an earring," he said.

"Whose earring?"

Eric paused, looked away then back at Galloway. "Leah Dunn's."

"And why was Leah Dunn's earring in your bed?"

"Uh-oh," I whispered to myself. My hand went to my jeans pocket where I'd stashed the cufflink I'd found at Leah's place. I'd forgotten I'd pocketed it.

"We're in love," Eric said, voice devoid of emotion.

"You were having an affair with Leah Dunn?" Galloway pressed.

"Yes."

"Did you kill Dean Ward?"

Wow. Direct. I liked it. I waited for Eric to respond.

"No. I did not kill Dean Ward."

"But you have to agree you have motive," Galloway said. "You're having an affair with his girlfriend. Maybe you wanted Dean out of the picture to have her all to yourself."

Eric snorted. "I've loved that woman for over three years. I could wait a little longer. She was going to leave him, and before you say *that's what they all say,* she was! But Dean was about to go down financially, and she didn't want to make a difficult situation worse. She wanted to see him through," Eric waved a hand around, "bankruptcy or whatever was going to happen. According to Leah, Moustache Craft Ales was about to go under."

I nodded. Moustache Craft Ales was in lousy shape all right, and what Eric was telling Galloway lined up with what Leah had told me. It also sounded as hinky as all get out. If you were no longer in love with a person, would you really hang around to help them in what could potentially be a long period of bankruptcy? Especially if you were already in a relationship with someone else? And Leah had indicated she was worried about Dean's state of mind, yet I'd seen nothing to indicate he was depressed, let alone potentially suicidal.

I shot a message off to Galloway.

*I think Leah Dunn is the killer.*

# 12

Galloway didn't even glance at his phone, completely ignoring my text. Resting my chin on my hand, I watched the rest of the interview. It didn't reveal anything I didn't already know. Eric kept claiming he was innocent, and I tended to believe him. Ending the interview, Galloway left the room. A second later, my door opened, and Galloway stood there, staring at his phone before raising his eyes. "You think Eric is innocent?" He quirked an eyebrow.

I nodded. "I do."

"Why?"

Excellent question. Because I kinda liked him and didn't like Leah? I didn't think Galloway would accept that as a good enough reason.

"Call it a gut feeling," I eventually said. He heaved a sigh, and I cut him off. "I know, I know, you can't arrest someone on a gut feeling. What happens now? With Eric?"

"We'll continue to hold him while we investigate. We'll take his prints and DNA, see if we can lift anything off the phone. Glad you had gloves on when you picked it up."

"I'm not a total rookie." I dug in my pocket and produced the cufflink, holding it out. "I know this isn't admissible as evidence, but I found it under Leah Dunn's bed. In her apartment."

Galloway took the cufflink and examined it. "Eric's, I assume."

"Right, but he told me they always met at his place. Why, then, was his cufflink under her bed?"

"Does it matter? Their affair has been uncovered. Her earring in his bed, his cufflink under hers."

"A little neat, don't you think?" I pressed.

Galloway tossed the cufflink in the air and caught it, keeping his gaze locked on me all the while. Gah, was it getting hot in here, or was it just me?

"Are you saying you think these items were staged?"

I shrugged. "Dunno. Perhaps? Maybe? Yes?"

Galloway held my gaze for a moment longer then closed the door and returned to the interview room. He held the cufflink out to Eric. "Is this yours?"

Eric leaned forward to take a look then nodded. "Yes. It's mine. Didn't even know it was missing. Where was it?"

"In Leah Dunn's apartment."

Eric reared back. "That can't be right."

"Why's that?"

"Because I've never been in her apartment. She and Dean leased that place after they got together. I've never set foot inside." He was pretty adamant about it.

"How, then, did your cufflink find its way under her bed?"

Eric crossed his arms. "No idea, but it wasn't me. I haven't worn those cufflinks for..." He looked at the ceiling while scouring his memory. "I can't recall. But a long time, probably more than a year ago."

"You're saying you haven't worn these cufflinks in a year?"

"Yes. They're dress cufflinks. Not standard attire for the bar. If that cufflink was found in Leah's house, then someone planted it there."

Bingo! I slammed my fist on the desk with a loud bang. Both Galloway and Eric jerked their heads in my direction. Oops. Cradling my smarting hand against my chest, I sat back in my chair while Galloway left the interview room once more.

The door opened.

I apologized before he could get a word in. "Sorry about that. I got a little excited."

"All of this is circumstantial. We need proof."

"How do you prove someone hasn't been inside someone else's house? That they haven't worn certain cufflinks in a year? That's impossible."

"Exactly. And we can't submit the cufflink as evidence."

"Because I took it from Leah's." Crap, crap, crappity crap. "We'll just have to find something else to prove Eric didn't do it." I was grasping at straws, and we both knew it.

"Actually, that's not my job," Galloway said. "It's my job to find out who killed Dean Ward, not prove someone didn't. I have to follow the evidence, and so far, it's pointing at Eric."

"Well, it's wrong," I huffed, crossing my arms. "And what about Jay Byrne, Dean's employee? Has he been brought in for questioning? I witnessed him selling drugs, and I'm more than happy to testify."

"We're looking for him."

"Looking for him? Are you saying you lost him?"

"I sent a patrol to pick him up from work, but he'd left early. He's not at home either. He'll turn up."

"Maybe he's in cahoots with Leah!" More likely Arlie Roberts, but something really didn't sit right with me when it came to Leah Dunn.

"Maybe we'll just follow the evidence instead of jumping to conclusions, hmm?"

He was right, of course. But that didn't mean I had to like it.

---

Standing in my kitchen, I made myself what I hoped was the last cup of decaf I'd ever have to consume and watched Bandit and Thor scarf down their kibble like they hadn't eaten in days.

"Guys, you had breakfast this morning. Cut the theatrics," I grumbled.

"Ignore her," Thor instructed Bandit. "She's just cranky because of the decaf."

"I like coffee," Bandit replied.

"You've never had coffee," Thor argued.

"I have."

"You haven't."

"I have."

"You haven't."

"Guys!" I protested, running a hand around the back of my neck.

"But I have had coffee. Remember that time when Mom left her coffee on the counter when someone was at the door, and we jumped up to see if there was any muffin left?"

I froze. What was I hearing? They both knew the counters were off-limits. Although I do recall finding one of Thor's hairs in my coffee cup before.

"Oh, yeah! You're right. I remember now." Thor nodded then began washing his face. "You stuck your paw in it."

"Not you too!" I squeaked, pulling a face.

"I like coffee," Bandit said.

"I can't believe I'm hearing this." I shook my head and eyeballed my cup suspiciously. Now I would have to be on the alert for Bandit and Thor from sticking their paws in my cup whenever my back was turned. Great.

"I can't either," Dean drawled from where he was sprawled on the couch. He and Ben had returned shortly after I arrived home, and I'd turned on the television to keep the two of them from bickering. If it wasn't my pets arguing, it was the ghosts. A headache began to throb behind my eyes, and I rummaged in my junk drawer for some Tylenol, then remembered I'd meant to pick some up today.

"Why is it you can talk to animals?" Dean persisted.

"Dunno," I grumbled, taking a seat at the breakfast bar and rolling my shoulders.

"Headache?" Ben asked sympathetically.

"Yeah."

He moved behind me and carefully held his hand an inch from my neck. The cool wave of air from his presence was soothing.

"Dean chose the wrong time to die," I sighed. "I'm finding it so hard to concentrate, to make sense of things while I'm off caffeine."

"Chin up. Today's the last day." Ben slapped me on the shoulder, only his hand passed right through me, and the pleasant cooling sensation was amplified tenfold into a glacial blast, making me flinch.

"Sorry." He moved away to take a seat in an armchair.

"No, you're not," I teased.

"I didn't choose to die," Dean interrupted. "It's

not like I decided, hey, I think I might get myself murdered today."

"Yeah, yeah." I waved a hand. "You know what I mean. Any other week and I would have solved this already. But this week, my brain is wrapped in molasses. There are so many layers and so many potential suspects."

"Let's talk it through," Ben suggested. "What have you got?"

"Galloway likes Eric Sullivan for it. Dean called a pay-as-you-go number, and that phone was found in a trash can at Eric's house. And, of course, there's the affair between Eric and Leah."

"Of course Eric did it," Dean huffed. "He's wanted me out of the way for a long time."

"And who could blame him?" I snapped. "But I don't think he killed you."

Dean sneered. "Of course you don't. This is why you're a PI and not a detective. You're a wannabe, pretending to be something you're not."

"You watch your mouth," Ben warned. "Remember you were found dead on her doorstep. You were coming to her, not the police."

"It's okay, Ben. I don't care what he thinks." It was true. Dean Ward could say what he liked, but I knew I was good at my job, and he was wrong. I had no desire to join the police force. Being a PI was my calling, only I hadn't known it until it was thrust upon me when Ben died. "Tell me, Dean, when did you tell Leah that marriage wasn't in the cards? That you didn't want kids? Was that…oh, let me see… about three months ago?"

Dean's head snapped around so fast I was surprised he didn't give himself whiplash. "Who told you that?"

"Who do you think?" It wasn't who he thought. It had been Eric, not Leah, who'd divulged that little nugget of information.

"Makes sense now." Ben was nodding. "Leah put the hard word on you. You'd been together for years. It was time to put a ring on it, huh? And you freaked."

"I didn't freak!" Dean blustered. "I just didn't want to get married. I don't see the point. Why buy the cow when you get the milk for free?"

"Are you even serious right now?" I shook my head. What a moron.

"What?" He seemed genuinely puzzled.

Ben saved me from answering. "Marriage isn't about sex. It's about sharing your life with the person you love. It's a choice. It's a higher level of commitment. It's a statement you want to make with your partner."

"Don't need a marriage certificate for that."

"No, you don't *need* a marriage certificate. But some people see it as a sign of commitment, coming together as a union… and clearly, that's where Leah was. She was ready for that next level of commitment."

"Rubbish." Dean sniggered. "I'd never suggested at any time in our relationship that marriage was in the cards."

"Yes, but when did you *specifically* tell her that?" I took a sip of my decaf and waited.

Dean's lips curled down. "Fine. It came up one night about six months ago. She said something about it being time to start thinking about kids, that she wasn't getting any younger, and that she'd like to be married first."

"And you disabused her of that possibility, I take it?" Ben asked.

"I told her that marriage wasn't necessary since we wouldn't be having kids." He shrugged matter-of-factly. Despite not liking Leah, I felt sorry for her at that moment. How awful to think the life you were building with someone wasn't what you thought it was.

"How did she take it?" I asked.

Dean shrugged. "Okay, I guess. She was pretty quiet for a few days, but then it was just life as normal."

I shared a look with Ben, and that's when it hit me. Of course, Leah killed Dean. That whole story she'd told Eric about waiting and helping Dean through his rough financial patch was a smoke-screen. Leah was a thirty-five-year-old woman who'd just discovered her partner did not want to have children with her. Her biological clock was running out of time. She wouldn't tie herself to Dean for longer than necessary. Why she didn't leave him then and there was beyond me, but the heart works in mysterious ways, and maybe at that point, she was still in love with the man. God only knows why.

Now she had Eric, utterly devoted and head over heels in love with her, ready to offer marriage and babies. Maybe she had the foresight to know that if she left Dean for Eric, he'd make their lives a living hell. He was that type of guy. So, why not get rid of him for good?

I nodded, convinced Leah was the killer. Now I just needed to prove it. Throwing back the rest of my decaf, I left the cup in the sink and grabbed my bag.

"Hey, where are you going?" Ben asked, following me.

"Moustache Craft Ales. I could use a drink."

"Great idea. Count me in." Dean joined us. And that is how, on the final day of my caffeine-free week, I was drinking at the bar with two ghosts.

# 13

Leah was pulling beers and joking with customers like her boyfriend hadn't just been murdered, a fact I found morbidly fascinating. But even I had to admit she was in her element. Her movements were fluid as she darted from one end of the bar to the other, brushing past the other bartender, Milo, with a quick smile, a kind word to every patron. Every now and then, she'd throw a glance my way, and I'd smile from my seat at the bar and raise my glass in a salute. Between Leah and Milo, they kept up with demand.

"Hey, Leah, is Jay around?"

I paused with my glass halfway to my mouth, watching as Megan Sullivan rushed up to the bar, her long black hair pulled up into a high ponytail. In black jeans and a black turtleneck top with no sleeves, she looked suitably bad-ass. And nowhere near the distraught young woman I'd seen at the hospital earlier. People of Firefly Bay sure did bounce back quickly from traumatic events.

"He went home sick," Leah said. "Milo's here to cover for him."

"Hey, Megan," I called, interrupting them. "How's Amy?"

Megan's ponytail danced around her shoulders as she swung her head toward me. "Oh, hi." Her smile was as fake as Leah's. "Yeah, she's fine. They're keeping her overnight for observation, but yeah, no ill effects."

I nodded and took a sip of cider, the bubbles tickling my nose. "That's good. It could've been worse. Did she tell you where she got the drugs?"

Megan's mouth thinned into a flat line, and her eyes narrowed. "Say it a little louder, why don't you? Like the whole town needs to know."

"Hey, now." Leah looked from me to Megan and then back at me, pointing a finger. "You'd better not be upsetting my customers, or I'll have to ask you to leave."

I blinked. "I am your customer. At least, I'm

buying drinks. She hasn't bought anything," I protested.

"Megan is a long-standing supporter of Moustache Craft Ales," Leah said proudly, and Megan tacked on, "Yeah."

"Fine. Sorry I spoke," I muttered, tilting my glass and finishing the cider.

"That was a bit hostile," Ben said from beside me.

"I know, right?" I replied out the corner of my mouth.

"Can I get you another, Audrey?" Milo appeared in front of me, hand poised, ready to take my empty glass. I was glad Leah was sticking to the other end of the bar and not serving me. By the daggers she was shooting in my direction, I wouldn't put it past her to slip a little something extra into my beverage.

"Yes, please."

"Make that two." Galloway slid onto the barstool at my left. "What are you drinking anyway?" He leaned in to kiss me, arm sliding around my waist to squeeze me tight before he settled more comfortably by my side.

"Pear cider." I held up two fingers to Milo, who nodded and began preparing our drinks. "So, Megan is in here a lot then?" I asked Milo while leaning into Galloway, my hand on his thigh.

"Yep." Milo glanced at the pretty brunette who leaned over the bar talking with Leah in hushed tones. "All the time. I think she has a crush on Jay. She's only ever here when he's working."

"Speaking of Jay," I turned to address Galloway, "has he turned up yet? Leah said he'd gone home sick."

Galloway shrugged. "Not yet. He's not at home, but that's not to say he isn't legitimately sick and gone to the doctor or even to the hospital."

Ben, to the right of me, leaned around to ask Galloway, "How did it go with the plate?" Only, of course, Galloway couldn't hear or see him.

"Shoot," I whispered.

"What?" Ben and Galloway said in unison.

Rather than answer them, I pulled out my phone and swiped through the photo gallery, bringing up the photo of the plate on the red hatchback. I showed it to Gallaway. "I saw this car earlier at the Firefly Bay Brewing Company. I'm pretty sure it's the one I saw here… earlier." I didn't want to say *drug deal* out loud in case Leah threw me out. "I was hoping you could run the plate?"

Galloway pulled out his own phone, squinted at mine, and typed something before sliding his phone away again. "I'm surprised you didn't run it yourself."

"Forgot." I shrugged. It had been a long day, and even as I thought it, a yawn overtook me.

Our drinks arrived in front of us, Galloway paid, and Milo hustled to serve a lumberjack-looking dude.

"Cheers." Galloway clinked his glass with mine and took a sip. "Hmm, this is good."

"Right?"

"Everything okay with Laura and the baby?" he asked, lowering his voice. I wasn't a fool. I heard the undercurrent of concern, the unspoken question. *How was I?*

"Laura and the baby are fine. Grace is perfect." I dutifully presented him with photos I'd taken at the hospital while visiting.

"And you? Are you okay? Laura said the birth may have seemed traumatic to you."

*Seemed* traumatic? Holy guacamole Batman, what an understatement. I met his look head-on. I could continue to lie and pretend everything was fine, or I could tell the truth. A truth that could impact our relationship. Potentially end it. Look at what happened between Leah and Dean. He didn't want kids, and now he was dead. Okay, an extreme example, but once you put the words out there, there's no taking them back.

"Babe." Galloway wrapped a firm hand around the nape of my neck and pulled me in close, resting his forehead against mine. "Whatever it is, you can tell me."

I sighed. "I know. It's just..." I trailed off. The words wouldn't come.

"You're not sure you want babies of your own?" he guessed.

You know, it's really hard to keep secrets when your boyfriend is not only a detective but also a very intuitive one.

"Is that a deal-breaker?" I whispered, neither confirming nor denying.

"No." He gave my neck a little squeeze, his fingers stroking just beneath my ear. "But it's also not something we have to decide right now. I love you and want to spend the rest of my life with you. If that includes children, great. I love kids. But if it doesn't, that's okay too."

My heart skidded and stuttered, did multiple somersaults, then took off racing again. "Are you proposing?" I gasped, lifting my head so I could look into his eyes.

"Not yet." He grinned then kissed me. Not a

chaste peck either. It was a passionate kiss that rocked my world. His kiss promised me the earth, moon, and stars and swept me off my feet.

"Urgh, gross. PDA between old people is revolting." Megan Sullivan practically gagged as she spat out the words.

Galloway broke the kiss. "Old people?" He snorted, glancing over his shoulder to watch as Megan flounced out of the pub, ponytail swishing with each step. Her words trailed behind her. "I'm going to find Jay."

Cupping Galloway's face in my hands, I drew his attention back to me. "She's going to find Jay," I said.

"I heard. And?" He was clearly bewildered by why that was important.

"If she has a crush on him like Milo suggested, then she's probably stalked him within an inch of his life. Who better to know where Jay is than a girl with a crush?"

Galloway's lips curled, and I was momentarily distracted.

"You're suggesting we follow her?"

I dragged my gaze from his mouth to his eyes. "Yes?" I breathed, forgetting what the question was.

Ben guffawed from beside me. "Forget it, guys.

She's long gone. And would you quit it with the dreamy looks already?"

"What?" I asked, turning my head slightly but keeping my eyes locked with Galloway's.

"What?" Galloway asked, brow furrowing.

"Oh. Ben's here," I explained, removing my hands from his face with a certain degree of reluctance.

Galloway looked over my shoulder, as if he could see Ben for himself. Bless him for trying. He always did that. Whenever I said Ben was around, Galloway would look for him. It was adorable.

"Maybe Ben could follow her, and we could enjoy our drinks?"

"I like it." A smile blossomed. After the week I'd had, some quality time with Galloway was precisely what I needed.

"Fine." Ben slid off the barstool, the frigid air at my back a testament to his presence. "Don't forget to ask Galloway about the liquor license for this place."

Shoot. I'd forgotten about that too. My memory was as effective as Swiss cheese. "Will do." It was then that I noticed Dean was no longer with us. A quick search of the bar showed no sign of him. "Where did Dean go?" I asked Ben.

"Don't know and don't care." He disappeared, and I turned my attention back to Galloway.

"We are officially ghost-free," I said.

"You mean I've got you all to myself?" His wolfish grin curled my toes, and I practically toppled off the bar stool.

"Well, you and an entire bar full of people, but yes."

"I say we finish our drinks and get out of here." The glint in his eye had me sighing in anticipation. Without hesitation, I tossed back the rest of my cider so fast bubbles shot up my nose, and I couldn't hold back the long, loud burp that followed.

"Oh, my giddy aunt!" I clapped a hand over my mouth, mortified. "I'm so sorry. That was rude. But damn if cider isn't incredibly gassy."

"That was impressive!" Galloway laughed and finished his own drink with no such theatrics.

"Sure was," Milo said in passing. "Put a trucker to shame."

Fantastic. Now I could add *burps like a trucker* to my resume. Life goals. Grabbing my hand, Galloway tugged me to my feet, and hand in hand, we headed home.

---

"Fitz… Fitz…" The persistent calling of my name had me grumbling in my sleep.

"Go 'way." Pulling the throw Galloway had pulled over us as we lay curled up together on the sofa up to my chin, I snuggled in closer to his warmth.

"Audrey Fitzgerald, wake up!" Ben touched my naked shoulder.

I shrieked, bolting upright and almost losing the throw. Madly grabbing it, I held it to my chest, covering myself. Galloway and I hadn't made it to the bedroom. We'd stumbled to the lounge, locked in a heated embrace, and that's where we'd stayed.

"Ben!" I hissed. "Do you mind?"

"What?" he protested. "I didn't see anything."

"That is not the point." I began searching for my clothes and managed to grab my T-shirt from the floor.

"What is it?" Galloway murmured sleepily. "Is it Ben? What does he want?" He yawned and stretched, distracting me with his abs.

"Quit drooling, Fitz," Ben teased.

I waved my finger in the air, indicating he needed to turn his back while I pulled the T-shirt over my head. Another quick rummage revealed my panties, and I pulled them on along with my jeans. Tucking the throw over Galloway's naked form, I stalked past Ben on my way to the kitchen.

"Okay, what's so important you had to disturb us?" I poured myself a glass of apple and mango juice, a new find that I'd recently discovered, and took a sip while I waited for Ben to reveal all.

"I was looking for Megan, as instructed—" he began when I cut him off.

"Did you find her? Did she find Jay?"

Ben cocked a brow. "If you'd let me finish?" he drawled.

I waved a hand for him to continue and sipped my juice.

"So, I didn't find her. Or Jay. Wherever he's hiding out is off the radar."

"Right. And you woke me up for that?"

"No. I woke you up because I came back here, and you were... busy... so I headed out again, down to number twelve. I'd seen a tradesman there earlier this week, so I figured I'd go check out what they'd had done."

Despite the tide of red I could feel creeping up my neck that Ben had walked in on Galloway and me mid... *you know*... I didn't find Ben's tale of number twelve's renovations particularly relevant.

Nor entertaining. I took another mouthful of juice and hoped he'd get to the point sometime soon. All the cider, and now juice, was making its presence felt in my bladder.

"So Noel and Noelene—"

"That's their names? Noel and Noelene?" I interrupted with a snort.

"Yes, Fitz. Noel and Noelene. Can I continue?"

"Please do."

"So, Noel and Noelene just had CCTV installed."

"Cool."

"And considering my house—your house, is at the end of a cul de sac…"

"Oh right, you figured their camera may have picked up traffic coming and going?" Now I could see his point.

"Exactly!" He beamed. "And lucky for us, the camera out front captures their driveway and part of the street."

"Tell me it was operational the night Dean died."

He nodded. "Yup, it was."

"And? Did you do your voodoo thing?" I mimicked the way he could hover his hand inside a cell phone and read the data.

"I did."

Jumping Jehosaphat, but he was taking the scenic route in getting to his point. "And?" I prompted.

"Well, it captured Dean driving past, nine minutes past midnight."

"Excellent. That gives us a time of death without waiting for the coroner's report. So, if he drove past Noel and Noelene's house at twelve-o-nine, then let's give him a minute or two to park and walk up to my door. So, he was probably killed around twelve-fifteen, give or take."

"Around that."

"Good work."

"Oh, there's more."

"There's more?" My eyebrows shot up.

"Immediately following Dean's car was a hatchback."

I held my breath.

"A red hatchback."

"Bingo!" I punched the air, startling Galloway awake.

"What's going on?" He sat up, primed for action, hands in a defensive pose against an as yet unseen threat.

"Sorry." I rushed over to him, sat on the edge of the sofa, and pinned the blanket to his hips in case he accidentally gave Ben an eyeful. "That was me. I'm talking with Ben."

Galloway stretched and nodded at the same time. "Can't believe we fell asleep down here."

"Right?"

"Guys? Can we focus, please?" Ben shook his head in mock despair.

"So, Ben went down to Noel and Noelene's at number twelve on a recon mission," I began, filling Galloway in on what he'd discovered.

"A red hatchback, huh? The same one you had me run the plate for?"

I shrugged. "Could be. Ben pointed out that, obviously, there is more than one red hatchback in Firefly Bay. Still, it can't be a coincidence that someone driving a red hatch bought drugs from Jay and was also seen leaving the scene of a crime."

"What time did it leave?" Galloway asked.

"It went back past Noel and Noelene's at sixteen past twelve."

"So, basically, the killer followed Dean here, must have parked behind him, ran up the lawn, plunged the knife in his back, ran back to their car, and left. Because that's a pretty tight timeframe."

"And why didn't Dean hear the car? Or see the headlights? The way he recounts it, he didn't hear or see anything. But you would, wouldn't you? It's the middle of the night, it's quiet, it's dark. You're going to notice a car engine. You're going to notice headlights piercing the dark."

"Do you think he's lying?" Ben asked, cocking his head.

Galloway stood up and wrapped the blanket around his hips. "I'm going to get a warrant for the CCTV footage," he said, searching through his pants for his phone.

"And the plate?"

"I already sent that through. I'll follow it up. We may be able to pull the plate from the CCTV footage and see if it's the same car."

Ten minutes later, he had answers. I was suitably impressed.

"The car in the photo you showed me belonged to Tamara Reed, an eighteen-year-old student," Galloway said after hanging up on his call with Firefly Bay PD. "She has no priors and no links that we can find to this case."

"What was she doing at a pub? She's underage."

"She was there to pick up her mom, who's a member of the book club. Her mom lost her license, DUI, so now her daughter is her chauffeur."

"So, someone spoke with her?" I pressed.

"Affirmative. It's not her, Fitz."

I chewed my lip. I'd been so sure that was the red hatch we were looking for. Now I was back at square one.

"Walsh did, however, run a search through DMV for red hatchbacks registered in Firefly Bay," Galloway continued.

*Genius! Why didn't I think of that? Oh, I dunno, probably because you're caffeine-deprived.*

I glanced at my smartwatch, only I wasn't wearing it. Then I remembered it was in my bag, waiting to be charged. Leaning forward from my position on the sofa, I picked up my cell and looked at the time on that instead. Just gone eleven pm. Less than an hour, and this stupid bet would be over.

"And?" I returned my attention to Galloway.

"Interesting result."

I barked out a laugh. "Come on, spill. You can't leave me hanging like this."

"Megan Sullivan owns a red hatch," he deadpanned.

"Wowsers," I whispered. Could Megan have killed Dean? Was she the one I saw buying drugs from Jay? Milo had said Megan was obsessed with Jay. Was buying drugs a ploy to get closer to him? My mind whirled a million miles a minute.

"How long will it take to get the CCTV footage from number twelve?"

Galloway chuckled. "Easy there, Fitz. It's late. We're waiting on a judge to sign the warrant. That probably won't happen until the morning. Why don't you go on upstairs and get some sleep? I'm going to drop into the station, see where we're at with everything, then crash at my place tonight so I don't disturb you."

"Call me in the morning," I demanded. "When you have the footage."

"Will do. Love you."

"Love you, too."

I walked Galloway to the door, gave him a thorough smooching goodnight, then closed the door behind him. Despite the nap I'd had on the sofa, I was, in fact, exhausted. And Galloway was right. There wasn't much to be done tonight. I'd start afresh tomorrow. Rested and fully caffeinated at long last.

Retrieving my phone from the coffee table, I said goodnight to Ben and headed upstairs, pausing in my bedroom doorway at the sight that greeted me. Bandit and Thor asleep together. Not on my bed, but in it. Spooning. With their heads side by side on the pillow, the covers tucked up under their arms. It was the most adorable thing I'd ever seen, especially the way Thor's chin rested on the top of Bandit's head and his paw around her shoulders, as if protecting her.

Pulling out my phone, I crept closer and snapped some photos then slid in beside them. At least they'd kept to one side of the bed and left room for me.

# 14

"Mom."

Now I knew why I was so tired and irritable. It wasn't just the coffee situation. It was from being constantly woken up.

"What?" I grumbled, turning my head only to come nose to nose with Bandit. I eased back a little, almost cross-eyed with the raccoon so close.

"There are strange noises."

"Whadda ya mean?" I yawned, tried to stretch, only something was pressing against my lower back, stopping me from rolling. I reached down, and my hands tangled in Thor's fur. So much for them sticking to their own side of the bed.

"There are noises. Outside," Bandit whispered. Only her whisper was thunderous.

"What kind of noises?" I sat up, dislodging Bandit. Thor barely moved.

"People noises." Bandit's head swiveled, and her ears twitched, her face intent as she listened again. I strained to hear anything.

"People noises?" What did that mean? "Like someone is outside?"

Bandit nodded, clutching at my arm. "Yes. Yes."

"Wake up, Thor, buddy, I've got to get up." I pushed the cat with my knee.

Lifting his head, he blinked at me with sleepy eyes. "Is it breakfast time?" he asked.

"No. Come on, scoot. I need to get up."

He stood, took his time stretching, then slowly padded to the foot of the bed, where he lay down again as if that short journey was exhausting.

"What's going on?" He yawned, eyes starting to drift closed.

"Bandit heard something outside. I'm going to investigate."

"Right." Eyes closed, he drifted off to sleep again.

"Thanks for the backup," I teased, throwing back the covers and swinging my legs out.

"I'll be your backup," Bandit assured me. "What's a backup?" she added.

I grinned and reached down to ruffle her fur.

"Nothing for you to worry about, Bandit. Why don't you stay here with Thor? I'll take a quick look downstairs."

I didn't want to alarm Bandit, but I was sure I'd heard the squeaky board on the stairs creak. Which meant someone was in the house. I tried to remember if I'd set the alarm after Galloway had left, but I'd been tired and may have missed it. Murphy's Law—the one time you forget, you get burgled. Tiptoeing across the room, I eased through my bedroom door, which I leave ajar for Bandit and Thor. Then I returned to retrieve my phone from the nightstand, which got me thinking... was my stun gun still in my purse?

Easing out the bedroom doorway once more, I made my way with the stealth of an elephant across the landing. At least I knew where the squeaky floorboards were and avoided each and every one. I hesitated at the top of the stairs, peering into the inky void below. Zero visibility. I held my breath and tried to listen over the ever-increasing beat of my heart. Was someone downstairs? I couldn't tell. Bandit had never woken me up about people noises before, so I believed her when she said she'd heard someone, but she'd said the noise came from outside. Was it my own overactive imagination that *thought* I'd heard the stair creak?

The tiny hairs on the back of my neck stood on end. It would be convenient if Ben were here right now. But he wasn't. He didn't hang around at night. He was off watching Netflix with the insomniacs or hanging with the night shift workers. Goodness knows where Dean was. I hadn't seen him in ages, and I wondered if the three spooky spirits were still following him around.

Then I heard it. A distinct scraping noise coming from downstairs. Keeping as close to the wall as possible, I hurried down the stairs. The front door was secure, the alarm off. Back to the wall, I eased down the hallway. The open plan kitchen, living, and dining areas were at the rear of the house, and the back wall was all glass. I rarely drew the blinds, preferring natural light, and right now, I was thankful for the moonlight shining in, easing the darkness. I paused as the hallway ended and the living room began. Keeping to the shadows, I popped my head around the corner.

Nothing. Had the intruder heard me and ducked for cover? Holding my breath, I waited. One minute. Two. My lungs burned, reminding me I needed oxygen. I released the breath I'd been holding with a whoosh and stepped into the living room, making a beeline for my purse that I'd spied sitting on a barstool at the kitchen bench.

Rummaging inside, my fingers wrapped around my stun gun, and I pulled it out, holding it in front of me, ready for action. I darted around the kitchen, ducked behind an armchair, and flung open the pantry door. Nothing. No one was here.

That's when I felt a breeze lift the hair at the nape of my neck, and slowly, I turned my head. The sliding door was open. Just a fraction but enough that I felt the breeze.

Was that the scraping noise I'd heard? Was it someone sliding the door closed? Only they'd left in a hurry and hadn't closed it the whole way. *Now* I was spooked. Flinging out my hand, I flicked on the lights, flipping every switch, so the entire bottom floor of my house was ablaze with light.

Crossing to the sliding door, I shut it properly and flicked the snib, then tested the handle to make sure it was securely locked. It was. Back to the front door, I doubled checked that too then went to set the alarm. Only the alarm didn't respond. I punched in my code. Nothing. No lights. It was as dead as a doornail.

Returning to the living room, I placed my phone

and stun gun side-by-side on the coffee table and sank onto the sofa, pondering what to do next. I was ninety-five percent sure someone had been in the house. Had they tampered with the alarm, or was it merely on the fritz? But the big question was, should I call Galloway now or wait until the morning? The big clock on the living room wall showed seven o'clock, but it had been stuck at seven for weeks because I kept forgetting to get batteries for it. My cell phone showed it was just past two in the morning.

I was still pondering when I curled up on the sofa, pulled the throw over my legs, rested my head on the cushion, and clutched the stun gun in my hands, lights ablaze. Which was unfortunate for Amanda, who, for some ungodly reason, had decided it was appropriate to let herself into my house at sparrows fart the following morning.

I'd been in a deep sleep on the sofa. I hadn't expected to awaken to find someone standing over me. Of course, I'd tasered her. Now I watched, horrified yet also fascinated, as she twitched on my living room floor.

"Amanda!" I surged to my feet, only I became tangled in the blanket and tripped, landing half on the floor, half on the coffee table with a painful thud.

"Ouch," I muttered, my knees smarting. The stun gun had slipped out of my hand and clattered onto the coffee table, teetering precariously on the edge. I reached out and repositioned it, holding my hands out as if commanding it to stay. Then I turned my attention back to my sister-in-law, who had thankfully stopped convulsing.

"Amanda." I crawled to her side, wincing at the hard floorboards beneath my already bruised knees. "You okay?"

"Mfrert?" She blinked, and a tiny bit of drool rolled down her chin. I pretended not to notice.

"Gah, you of all people should know better than to sneak up on me," I grumbled, feeling bad that I'd tasered her and then mad that I felt bad because it *wasn't my fault*. "It's okay. The effects will wear off soon. You'll be fine." I watched her for a minute, made sure she was breathing okay before I pushed myself to my feet. "Once you can speak, maybe you can tell me what you're doing in my house? The doors were locked. How did you get in?"

She tried to answer, but her words were nothing more than garbled noise.

"Hold that thought," I told her. "I've gotta pee."

On my way back from using the downstairs bathroom, I noticed a lone key placed precisely on the dresser in the hallway. It hadn't been there last night.

"Do you have a spare key to my house?" I yelled, storming down the hallway to the living room.

Amanda had dragged herself off the floor and into an armchair. Her usually sleek hair had a slight frizz to it, and I bit back a smile. *Serves you right.*

Then I spotted the two takeout coffee cups on the breakfast bar. Maybe I'd forgive her after all.

Crossing to them, I picked one up and took a sniff. Urgh. Green tea. Gross. I put it back and picked up the other one, taking a tentative whiff. Ahhh. Coffee. I took a sip, hoped for her sake it wasn't decaf, then carried her green tea over and placed it on the coffee table. I knew from experience that her limbs would probably still be tingling. Best not give her a hot beverage to hold just yet.

"Thanks for the coffee. I'm assuming it's not decaf?"

She shook her head.

"Great. First caffeine hit in seven days. I win the bet, by the way, and you know what that means?" I didn't give her time to answer. "It means no more interference in my life. So, shenanigans like letting yourself into my house have got to stop. Where did you get a key anyway?"

"I had one cut," she admitted, clearing her throat.

I let that sink in, trying my best not to lose my cool. I knew Amanda did what she did out of love, but man, she could be *so* frustrating at times.

"Boundaries, Amanda. That's overstepping," I finally said.

"I understand."

I cocked my head and watched as she shook her hands. Did she understand? I hoped so. Maybe getting unexpectedly tasered had done the trick.

"What are you doing here anyway, at—" I picked up my phone to check the time. Should have known. "—six am?"

"I thought I'd bring you a coffee as a way of saying congratulations, you won. I honestly didn't think you could do it."

I narrowed my eyes and considered tasing her again.

"Well, I have. The bet is over. I won." It felt good to say it because the last week had been utter hell. Already, the euphoria I usually experience from consuming caffeine was returning. I could practically feel my synapses firing. After two mouthfuls, I was buzzing.

"Why were you sleeping down here with the lights on?" she asked.

"I thought I had an intruder. I was keeping guard."

"An intruder?" She gasped. "Why didn't you call the police?"

"I had it under control." Plus, I had every intention of calling Galloway. In the morning. I just hadn't expected Amanda to let herself into my house at such an ungodly hour.

"Audrey, I really do think—" she began, but I cut her off, waggling a finger.

"Uh-uh-ah. No interference."

"Surely I can give my opinion?" She huffed.

"Nope." I shook my head. "Your opinion involves telling me what to do." I leaned forward, resting my elbows on my knees, rethought that position as the bruised flesh protested, and instead bent farther to place my drink on the coffee table. "I know you mean well," I began. Her mouth opened, but again, I cut her off. "Let me finish, please." She lapsed into silence, watching me.

"I know you mean well, but Amanda, I'm a grown adult. I've been taking care of myself for years. Yes, I'm clumsy. I've always been clumsy. I'll always be clumsy. You see it as an affliction. I see it as a quirk. I don't need to be fixed... I'm not broken."

"But—"

"No." I stood my ground. This had to stop.

Her lips thinned into a straight line, but she didn't say a word, just reached for her green tea and took a sip. The next five minutes were spent in silence, and it was blissful. Mostly because I had coffee again. A close second was the fact that Amanda wasn't speaking.

Eventually, she sighed and placed her now empty cup on the coffee table. "I should go," she said.

"You want me to call Dustin to come get you? You just got tased. That stuff rattles you. You probably shouldn't drive."

"I didn't drive. I jogged."

I blinked. "You jogged here? Carrying two drinks? How did you manage that? And how come they were still hot?"

She waved a hand. "I jogged to the café," she clarified. "Then caught an Uber here."

Oh, that made more sense. It also explained why she was decked out in activewear.

"So, you want me to call Dustin then?"

"No, thank you. I'll just call another Uber. Madeline and Nathaniel will still be asleep, and he'll have to get them up if he's going to come get me."

She ordered her ride, and once it was on its way, I walked her out, deliberately picking up the key she'd had cut and left on the hallway dresser and holding it up between my finger and thumb. "I'll keep this."

Her lips flattened again, but she didn't say a word, just lifted her hand with a wave and let herself out.

# 15

"Well, Ben was right," Galloway said. "It was definitely a red hatchback that followed Dean's car down your street the night he died."

I squished my phone between my ear and my shoulder while I wrangled my keyboard into place. It wasn't in its usual position, which led me to believe that whoever had been in my house last night had been in my office. Touching my things. Urgh, just the thought of it made my skin crawl.

"And? Could you see the plate?"

"No. Wrong angle. But we did get a partial of the driver."

"Megan?" I guessed.

"Actually, he or she was blonde."

My head straightened, and the phone, released from its grip, clattered to the desk. I picked it up. "Sorry 'bout that. Dropped the phone."

"Everything okay?"

"I think someone was in my house last night?" *Liar!* I *knew* someone was in my house last night.

"What? Why didn't you call me? Are you okay?"

"I'm fine, I'm fine. Bandit heard them and woke me up. I think they may have heard me on the landing and hightailed it out of here before I busted them."

"Has anything been taken?"

"Not that I can see. The only disturbance is in my office—the keyboard isn't where it usually is, but to be fair, that could have been Bandit and Thor. They do like to sprawl out across my desk."

"I'm coming over."

"It's really not necessary," I protested but was secretly pleased. In all honesty, I was a little rattled someone had been in my house while I'd been upstairs sleeping.

"No arguments," Galloway insisted. "I'm on my way."

I decided the least I could do was make us both breakfast, so when Galloway arrived, I was cooking up a storm in the kitchen. Bacon was sizzling, eggs were burning, and the toast had flung itself out of the toaster in some sort of bid for freedom and catapulted itself to the floor where Thor and Bandit sniffed at it disdainfully, refusing to touch the charred offering.

I took a sip of my third coffee and dazzled him with my smile.

"You look happy!" he said, ignoring the smoke hovering in the air.

"I am. Look!" I lifted my cup. "Coffee."

"How many of those have you had?"

"Does it matter?"

"Not at all." Then he clocked the stun gun on the coffee table and stilled. "Anything you want to tell me?"

I opened my mouth, but before I could say anything, the smoke detector went off. Turning off the burners, I hurried to the back door and slid it open, fresh air billowing in to disperse the smoke. Galloway stood under the detector with a towel and fanned it until the alarm eventually stopped.

"Good grief, you attempting to cook again, Fitz?" Ben appeared, waving his hand in front of his face.

"Har har." I piled two plates with burned eggs and extra crispy bacon, put more bread into the toaster, and dialed it down so it wouldn't burn, angling it so when it was done, the toast would hopefully land on the counter rather than the floor.

"Good, now that you're here, I can tell you both at once." I carried the plates to the dining table, returned for cutlery, then sat opposite Galloway, who, bless his heart, was eyeing the plate of food with feigned enthusiasm.

"Ben's here?" Galloway asked, attempting to cut the bacon, only it crumbled beneath his knife and fork. Giving up, he used his fingers, the crunch loud.

"Mmmm." I followed suit, picking up a strip of bacon and gnawing on the end. It really was crunchy. And chewy. Possibly inedible.

"So, last night, I had an intruder. I didn't actually see anyone, but I heard them. Or at least, I think I did. The back door was partially open. And the alarm isn't working."

"It isn't?" Ben shot off to examine the alarm while Galloway took a mouthful of burned eggs and valiantly tried to swallow.

I reached out and grabbed his wrist. "You don't have to eat them. I know I'm not the world's best cook, but usually, I can manage bacon and eggs. But I know this is a red hot mess. I won't be offended if you don't eat it."

"Why is your stun gun on the coffee table?" he asked around his mouthful of rubbery goodness.

"I got it out while I was checking for the intruder." I shrugged. "And then I accidentally tased Amanda," I added.

He spat his eggs out all over his plate then looked horrified. "I'm so sorry." He choked.

I laughed. "It's okay. I've done way worse." He made a move as if to continue eating the horrific breakfast I'd served up, so I whipped the plate away just as the toaster popped. This time the toast shot up into the air and landed on the counter. Yay for small wins.

"How about toast?" I suggested, carrying our plates back to the sink.

"Let me help. While I do this, you tell me how you accidentally tased Amanda," he said from behind me. After slathering the toast in butter, he handed me a piece while I told him about what had transpired with Amanda earlier.

Ben had returned, and if ghosts could have peed, he'd have peed himself laughing.

"You got the key back, though?" Ben finally composed himself enough to ask.

"Yes. I got the key back. And I think, maybe, finally, Amanda and I have reached an understanding." Lordy, but I hoped so. "How did it go with the alarm panel? Have I blown a fuse or something?"

Ben sobered. "Bad news. Wires have been cut."

"What?" I squawked.

"What? What is it?" Galloway had had his back to me while he put on more toast but quickly turned, his eyes darting around the room.

"Ben just told me the wires to my alarm system have been cut."

"Show me," Galloway demanded.

"Show me," I repeated to Ben. The three of us bundled outside to view where some lowlife had indeed snipped the wires.

"Whatcha all looking at?" Dean asked, arriving to find us gathered around the plastic box attached to the side of my house.

"Someone cut the wires to my alarm system," I told him. "Where have you been anyway?"

He shrugged. "Around."

I studied him for a moment. He seemed different. Agitated. Not sure if I was imagining it or not, I herded everyone back inside. Despite no one living next door, I didn't want to risk being seen talking to ghosts if someone happened to walk by.

"Right. Dean, let me bring you up to speed. We have CCTV footage of a red hatchback following you here the night you died. Did you notice another car?"

He shook his head. "No." But he wouldn't meet my eyes. Was he lying? I was pretty sure he was, but I didn't know why.

"Pretty hard to miss," Galloway offered up, despite not being able to see or hear Dean. "Dead of night. A car engine. Headlights. We know the headlights were on. Saw them in the CCTV footage."

"Care to revise your answer, Dean?"

Nothing. He remained tight-lipped.

"The driver was blonde," I prodded.

He visibly jerked. He knew! He knew it was Leah all along.

Which is precisely what I said out loud. "You don't have amnesia at all." I pointed at him, voice rising. "You knew all along it was Leah who killed you."

His arms flailed around as if he didn't know what to do with them before yelling, "Fine! Okay, I admit it. I suspected it was Leah. I did hear a car and saw a flash of headlights, but they stopped before they reached your house, so I figured it was a neighbor returning home."

"What made you suspect it was Leah then?"

"A strand of blonde hair out of my peripheral

vision. Before I could turn, the knife was in my back, and I was face down on your lawn."

It was my turn to throw my arms in the air. "Why on earth didn't you just tell us—me—in the first place and save all this hassle?"

"Because I didn't want to believe it. I didn't want to believe that Leah could do that to me."

I bit my lip. "Fair enough."

Galloway nudged me. "What's happening?"

"Dean says he saw a strand of blonde hair in his peripheral vision right before he was killed. He didn't say anything to us because he didn't want to believe his girlfriend was a murderer. Oh, and he did hear a car engine and notice headlights, but they stopped before my place, and he thought it was a neighbor coming home."

"Since the whole memory thing is bogus, why was he coming to see you?" Galloway asked.

"Excellent point." I crossed my arms and glared at Dean. "Well?"

He sighed. "I wanted you to find out who was dealing drugs in my pub. That number you found on my phone? I found it scribbled on a napkin, along with an empty baggie, shoved in the bin in the men's bathroom."

"Who answered? When you rang the number?" Ben asked.

"No one. There was silence, like they were waiting for me to speak first."

"And did you?"

"Other than *hello? Anyone there?* No. I figured they were waiting on a code word or something so as not to reveal their identity, so I hung up. That's when I decided to bring what I knew to you and let you figure it out."

I repeated what Dean had said to Galloway.

"So, Dean suspected someone was selling drugs out of Mustache Craft Ales and wanted to hire you to find out who it was. But he was killed before he could do so." He paused, looking at me but not really looking at me, more his eyes were pointed my way, but his mind was a million miles away. "Did Dean tell anyone of his suspicions? Clearly, the killer—who we assume is behind the drugs—knew that he knew and wanted to silence him from blowing the horn."

"I didn't tell anyone, no," Dean said.

"He says no," I translated.

"So, it had to be someone in the bar that night," Galloway surmised.

"It has to be Leah," I replied. "She probably knew

Megan was hot for Jay and was mooning after him like a lovesick puppy. So, she *borrows* her car, follows Dean, kills him, takes the car back, and no one is the wiser."

"Why protect Jay, though? Unless she's involved too."

"Good point. So? We're going to talk to her, right?"

"Correct. But, before we go, maybe you need to feed the animals?" He glanced toward the food bowls, and I followed his gaze to see Thor sprawled face-first in his kibble bowl, asleep.

"Man, but he does the cutest things," I whispered, whipping out my phone and snapping another shot. "I'm going to send this into that funny pet pics competition."

"Oh, yeah? What's that?"

"It's a competition run by Animal Antics. It's a fundraiser for a shelter. The winner gets an all-expenses paid tropical holiday—with their pet—to Wild Haven Lagoon."

Galloway grinned. "Nice."

"Not that I expect to win, but he's so cute." I bent and scratched under Thor's chin. He immediately rolled over and began purring before cracking one eye and muttering, "Where's my breakfast?"

After filling Thor and Bandit's bowls with their morning ration of kibble, I joined Galloway in his car and headed to Leah's house. Only she wasn't home. We tried Eric's house on a hunch, and sure enough, there was her car in the driveway next to Megan's red hatch.

"No need to sneak around anymore, huh?" I said as I climbed out of the car and walked by Galloway's side to the front door.

"Guess not," he said, ringing the bell then stepping back to wait.

Megan answered the door, looked us up and down, and curled her lip. "What?" She sneered. I shot a glance at Galloway, who'd produced his badge.

"Megan Sullivan? I'm Detective Kade Galloway. This is Audrey Fitzgerald. Can we come in?"

The sneer transformed into a flat-lined grimace. "If you have to." She spun away, leaving us to follow.

"What do you want?" She stood in the center of the living room, arms crossed over her chest.

I shook my head. So much angst for such a young person.

Her dark hair was loose, falling dead straight around her shoulders and down her back. No lipstick today, but her eyes were lined with black kohl, and her mini skirt and crop top, coupled with

Doc Martins—who wears Doc Martins these days?—made her look like a throw-back from the eighties. They say fashion trends tend to come back in, and looking at Megan, I'd say they were right.

"I take it the red hatch in the driveway is yours?" Galloway asked.

"Yeah. So?"

"Does anyone else drive it?"

She tossed her hair over her shoulder. "No. Why?"

"We have CCTV footage of a blonde person driving your car on the night of the eighteenth."

She frowned, eyes narrowing. "No way." But the bite was gone from her words, and you could practically see the cogs turning. Then, "That little cow!"

She stormed out of the room shouting, "Leah! You stole my car, you bi—"

"Hey!" Eric shouted from the landing. "What's with the shouting? What's going on?"

"Your piece of trash girlfriend stole my car, that's what," Megan fumed, pausing halfway up the stairs.

Leah appeared behind Eric. "What's going on?"

Galloway and I stood in the foyer and watched.

"You stole my car." Megan was moving again, taking the remainder of the stairs two at a time and closing in on Leah fast.

Leah strategically placed Eric between the two of them. "I did not steal your car. It's in the driveway. I don't know what you're even talking about."

"Not now, idiot," Megan cussed. "The eighteenth." She snapped her head around to glare at Galloway. "I assume that's the night Dean died, right?"

"Correct."

Leah gasped. "I did not take your car. Why would I? I haven't even been in your car."

"Liar," Megan spat. "No one believes you anyway. You're nothing but a cheater."

"Megan," Eric pleaded, resting his hand on Megan's shoulder only to have her shrug it off. "Leah didn't take your car."

She snorted. "How would you know?"

"Because she was with me that night."

Megan jerked her chin in the air. "Prove it."

I was all ears. *Go ahead, Eric, prove it.* Despite he and Leah being each other's alibi, neither of them could prove it.

"Actually, I can prove it," Leah said. Eric looked at her over his shoulder and gave a slight shake of his head. "What? It's true. Look, I know this isn't how we wanted things to go, but the truth is out there now, and it may as well be on our terms."

"Are you saying you have evidence that you and

Eric were together the night of Dean's death?" Galloway had his official voice on, and I loved it. All I needed now was for him to whip out his cuffs, and I'd be in heaven.

"Here." Leah cautiously stepped around Eric and Megan, as if expecting the young woman to lunge for her throat at any second. When Megan stayed rooted to the spot, Leah hurried down the stairs, phone outstretched. Galloway took it, and I craned my neck to get a look. Ohhh, salacious. A bedroom selfie. Leah and Eric in bed together. Thankfully, the important bits were covered.

"That could have been taken at any time," I pointed out.

"But it wasn't. It was that night. Check the metadata."

"I'm going to have to keep your phone for the time being while we corroborate your story." Galloway tucked the phone into his pocket.

"That's fine."

"Is that all?" Eric asked, arm around his daughter's shoulders as they looked down at us from the landing.

"No, it isn't," Galloway replied. "Megan, I'm going to have to impound your car so forensics can go over it."

"You can't do that!" she protested, back ramrod straight.

"Your car was seen at the scene of a crime. If it wasn't you driving it and it wasn't Leah, who was it?"

"I don't know."

"And that's why we need forensics. They can pull fingerprints, hairs, help us to identify who was behind the wheel."

"This is so unfair." She flounced off, and a second later, a door slammed.

Eric headed down the stairs to join us in the foyer. "Let's take this into the living room, shall we?"

Galloway led the way, I brought up the rear. If the metadata on the phone checked out, then it hadn't been Leah driving Megan's car.

Once in the living room, Eric clasped hands with Leah, their fingers intertwined. "You're saying the killer stole Megan's car and what? Drove it to kill Dean?"

"Megan's car was following Dean the night he died, yes." Galloway nodded.

"Why didn't you show us that photo before now?" I asked Leah. "Knowing it could clear both your names?"

She shrugged. "Like I wanted this out there. It's private."

"I could charge you with impeding an ongoing investigation," Galloway said. The color drained from Leah's face. "Is there anything else you're not telling us?"

She shook her head vehemently. "No. I came here from work. Dean was still at the pub—he often stays late by himself, doesn't come home until the early hours, so I knew I had an hour or two before I had to be home."

We were interrupted by Galloway's phone. Glancing at the screen, he shot me a look before swiping to answer. "Galloway."

I couldn't hear what was being said, but I didn't miss the way his lips compressed into a hard line, nor the weary shake of his head. "Yeah, okay. Thanks for the update. Station someone at the hospital."

He hung up, took a second to gather his thoughts, then said to Eric and Leah, "We believe the killer had access to Megan's car. I'll be sending a tow truck to pick it up. Please make sure she doesn't drive it in the meantime. I'll also have our tech team run the metadata on your phone. I'll make sure you get it back as soon as possible."

"You don't think Megan is involved, do you?" Eric asked, his face anguished.

I imagined Megan was quite the handful. As a

single dad, it must be challenging, especially now word was out he had a new woman in his life.

"We can't rule it out."

I looked from him to Eric and back again. Was Megan involved? I hadn't thought so, other than her crush on Jay, but maybe she knew more than she was letting on. But that was just on the drugs front. I sincerely doubted she was involved in Dean's death. That seemed an impossible leap.

Once we were back in the car, I clicked my seat-belt and asked, "What was that about the hospital? Has something happened?"

"Jay Byrne was just dumped outside of emergency."

"What? Is he okay?"

"He's unconscious. Badly beaten."

I blinked. *Wow*. "The plot thickens."

# 16

"Oh my gosh, Bandit, what happened?" I rushed to scoop her into my arms, my fingers brushing away blood-matted fur from her forehead.

"Our new neighbors don't like me," she wailed, tucking her head between my neck and shoulder and snuggling in as if she couldn't get close enough.

"They hurt you?" My temper rose. How dare someone hurt such a beautiful, defenseless creature.

"They threw a rock at her," Thor said, sitting at my feet, his orange eyes full of concern for his friend.

"Here, let me look. We'll need to get that cleaned up."

“I don’t want to go to the vet!” Bandit screeched, digging her claws into my back.

“Relax, relax. Let me see first, okay? There’s not too much blood. Let me just clean it with a washcloth first. It’s probably just a scratch.” If animals were like humans, head wounds bled like the devil.

Carrying her into the bathroom, I sat her on the vanity, ignored the blood she’d smeared over me, and ran a washcloth under the faucet before gently dabbing at the cut just above her eye.

“There… it’s not that bad. Just a scratch,” I soothed once I’d surveyed the damage. It was true. A one-inch scratch above her right eye. Still, it didn’t matter how nasty her wound was. What mattered was that someone—my new neighbor apparently—had thrown a rock with the intent to hurt. And that, I couldn’t stand for.

“You two stay here. I’m going to have a word with our neighbor.”

“Maybe you should wait for Galloway,” Thor suggested. “These people are strange.”

“They can’t be any stranger than Mrs. Hill.” I sniffed, remembering my run-in with the elderly woman and her poisoning me with Crimson Bark.

“When did they move in, anyway? I never saw a moving truck.”

Thor twitched an ear. "Dunno. Lots of funny noises and smells, though."

"Yucky smells," Bandit chimed in, nodding.

"And they hide when they see you," Thor added.

"What? They hide when they see me?"

"Mmhmm." Another ear twitch. "They keep the blinds closed all the time, but when your car approaches, they turn off the lights too."

"How odd."

"Maybe send Ben over there first?" Thor suggested. He was really concerned with me going over alone. I guess the poor guy was traumatized from my near-death experience the last time I'd set foot inside that house.

"He can't get in, though, remember? Mrs. Hill had some sort of sigil or spell on the house, and even though she doesn't live there anymore, he still can't get in."

"Maybe we need to kill her to break the spell," Thor said to himself, and I gaped at my cat in shock. Had I heard him right? He noticed me looking at him askance and twitched his nose. "Joking."

Was he, though? Anyway, it was a moot point. Mrs. Hill no longer lived there. *Not* that I had any intentions of killing her.

"What's up?" Ben appeared, noticing the blood on

my neck and shirt, and immediately went into over-protective mode. "Who hurt you? Where are they? I'll make them wish they'd never been born!"

"Calm down. It's not my blood. It's Bandit's." I nodded toward the raccoon, now standing on her hind legs nosing about in the overhead vanity, her trauma forgotten.

"What happened?"

"Apparently, we have new neighbors, and one of them threw a rock at Bandit," I explained. Just saying it out loud had my blood boiling. "I'm about to go over there and give them a piece of my mind."

What followed was a ten-minute debate with a cat and a ghost on the merits of approaching our new a-hole neighbor without backup. In the end, I relented and slid the stun gun in the back of my waistband. Pulling my T-shirt over it, I could only hope I didn't accidentally zap myself in the butt.

"I guess I should change my shirt," I said, rinsing the bloody washcloth and wiping at my neck.

"Nah, leave it. It adds impact," Thor said, eyeing the bloodstains with approval.

"I'm not going over there to threaten them," I protested. "More to educate them on how to treat animals, and that Bandit isn't wild, she's my pet."

"Maybe wait for Galloway," Ben said, not for the first time. "Where is he anyway?"

"At the hospital. Someone beat up Jay Byrne pretty bad. He's waiting for him to wake up to get a statement. Anyway, I don't need to wait for Galloway. I'm a grown woman who can take care of myself. Guys, this is just a new neighbor that I'm going to introduce myself to—and point out that there are laws against animal cruelty. Geez, have a little faith."

I headed toward the front door, my entourage in tow. I stopped with my hand on the knob. "Thor and Bandit, it might be best if you stay inside. Out of sight. Just for now, until I've had a chance to get a feel for these people."

"Good idea," Ben agreed. "It just makes me uneasy because I can't come with you."

"That's not what makes you uneasy. What makes you uneasy is that you can't get in at all. You can't scout ahead to see if I'm walking into danger. That's what's bothering you."

"You're probably right." He sighed.

"I'm always right." I grinned then slipped out the front door. Crossing the driveway, I set foot onto their front lawn and stopped, memories crashing in of the last time I was on this lawn. Mrs. Hill had poisoned me and had been intent on my demise. If it hadn't been for Ben, Thor, and Galloway, I'd be toast.

Shoving that thought aside, I kept moving. This was ridiculous. They were just people. New neighbors. I wondered where they'd come from. The house had sat empty for all these months, no for sale sign or anything. Had they bought it or leased it. Young or old? How many of them? Thor had said they were quiet and turned out the lights when I was around, which was bizarre, but maybe they were intensely private?

Reaching the front door, I raised my fist and pounded then stepped back to wait. Nothing. No sounds of footsteps from within. No sounds of anything. If Thor and Bandit hadn't told me someone was living here, I would have thought the place was empty. And that's when an icy trickle made its way between my shoulder blades, and the hairs on my arms stood on end. What better place to set up a drug lab than in an empty house?

Sliding my phone out of my back pocket, I dialed Galloway. It went to voicemail, and I hesitated before blurting in a whisper, "I'm next door. My next door, not your next door. Thor and Bandit say I have new neighbors, and one of them threw a rock at Bandit and hurt her—she's fine—" I quickly added. "Anyway, I came over to... *introduce myself,* and this thought just popped into my head. What if—" Beep. Darn. Ran out of time. I rang back, waited for his voicemail to kick in before continuing, "What if someone is using Mrs. Hill's old place to make drugs? What do you call making drugs? Cooking? Baking? Growing? Although surely I'd smell it if it were marijuana. Although Thor and Bandit did say funny smells, that could be anything really, couldn't it? Anyway, I'm next door. No one is home, so I'm—" Beep.

Sliding the phone into my back pocket, I retreated to my own house.

"Well? What did they say?" Ben asked, pacing back and forth on my driveway.

"Nothing. No one's home. But I had a thought."

"Uh-oh."

Ignoring him, I continued, "What if someone is using next door as a drug den? The place has been empty for almost a year."

"We'd have noticed. Wouldn't we?"

"Not necessarily." Although it pained me to admit it. How embarrassing to be a PI and have a drug lab erected in the house next door, and you had no idea.

"Look, I could be way off, but I'm going to check it out."

I darted down the path running the length of my house to the wooden gate leading into next door's back garden. The same gate that had a sigil burned into it that seemed to stop Ben from entering. I'd tried scraping the sigil off, burning it, painting over it, yet the darn thing would not budge. Goes to show Mrs. Hill was more of a witch than anyone thought.

"Fitz! Fitz!" Ben hissed, chasing after me, ricocheting off the invisible forcefield. "You can't go in there."

"Ahh, but I can!" I darted across the back garden, zigging and zagging, ducking behind shrubs just in case someone was actually inside, keeping guard. I crouched beneath a crab apple tree and lifted the fake rock nestled at the base of the trunk. "Thor told me about Mrs. Hill's spare key," I stage whispered, waving the key in the air.

Dashing to the back door, I plastered myself against the wall, all the while the theme of Mission Impossible playing in my mind. Sliding along the wall, I leaned around and peeked through the glass panel on the back door. Couldn't see a thing. I pressed back against the wall again then risked another look. Still nothing. I pressed my ear to the window to listen. Not a sound.

As quietly as possible, I slid the key into the lock and turned, the cylinder's rumble sounding impossibly loud. The door opened with a creak, and I froze on the threshold. Nothing happened. I stepped inside and sucked in a breath. The air smelled stale. Old. As if no one had opened a door or cracked a window in, oh, I don't know, a year. Slowly, I made my way inside. There was nothing there. Literally nothing. The dining room was empty, the pictures that had hung on the wall gone. No furniture, no knickknacks, no doilies. The blinds and curtains were pulled, blocking out the light, but there was enough to see by, and what I could see told me no one lived here. Thor and Bandit had it wrong.

I almost left then and there, but something pulled me toward the front bedroom. The room where Mrs. Hill had etched a pentagram into the floor and had prepared to make a blood sacrifice out of me. I couldn't resist. One last look, then I'd lock up and be gone. Whoever had thrown a rock at Bandit didn't live here. It must've been someone walking by.

My fingers wrapped around the doorknob, and my heart skipped a beat as sweat trickled down my back. "Why are you even doing this to yourself?" I whispered, turning the knob. It was dark inside the room. Darker than the rest of the house, and I squinted to see. Was the pentagram still on the floor? I supposed it had to be. She'd carved it with a knife. They'd have to replace the floorboards to get rid of it, and I hadn't seen any construction workers since she'd... left.

I frowned at how very dark it was and was reaching for my phone to use the flashlight app when I bumped into something. Was that a chair? It made a screeching noise as it scraped across the floor. Why was there furniture in this room when the rest of the house was empty?

It all happened so fast, yet in slow motion. I was already spooked, holding my breath until I felt dizzy, so when a hard object was pressed into my back, and a voice growled in my ear, "Hold it right there," my reaction was instinctive and adrenaline-fueled. I grabbed my stun gun, had the trigger compressed and the prongs in firm contact with whoever was behind me before I'd even turned around.

I heard the zing of the taser, the *urgh* of my assailant, felt the whoosh as something flew by my head, then heard an almighty crash as they fell to the floor. Bringing my taser around to the front of my body, I gripped it with both hands and turned, aiming it at where I thought my attacker was on the floor. Only, of course, it was so darn dark I could only see a black shape. I took a step backward, reached for the light, flicked it on and off a few times, but nothing happened. Of course. No electricity. Which again didn't make sense because Thor and Bandit said they turned the lights off when I was around. There had to be a power supply here somewhere.

I shuffled back some more, toward the window, and that's when I noticed it was covered in black plastic, secured at the edges with tape.

Reaching up, I tugged it away, and light flooded the room, highlighting the dust motes. And Megan Sullivan, who was struggling to sit up.

"Megan!" I gasped, unable to believe my eyes. She wasn't looking at me, rather at something on the floor near my foot. I glanced down, blanching when I saw what she was looking at. A gun. That's what had poked me in the back. That's what had sailed past my head when I'd tased her.

Shoving the stun gun back into my waistband, I bent and picked up the gun, trying not to let my hands shake. I aimed it at her. "Don't move. Shuffle up and put your back against the wall," I commanded.

"Make up your mind," she sneered, her voice as cold as ice, her eyes emotionless. "Don't move or put my back against the wall. I can't do both."

I gestured with the gun. "Don't get smart. Move back, then put your hands on your head." I had no idea what I was doing.

"You've watched too many cop movies," she grumbled but obliged. Keeping one eye on her, I glanced around the room. One long trestle table was pushed along the far wall. On it sat scales, small empty plastic bags, and three larger bags with different colored pills in each. Not a lab though. Megan wasn't cooking meth here, but she was undoubtedly distributing something.

"You're the one selling drugs?"

"Hello, Captain Obvious."

Hey, that was my line! I frowned, confused. "But I saw you buying drugs from Jay."

"Did you, though?"

"Well... yeah... I did."

"God, you're so stupid." She sneered, voice dripping disdain.

"Well, maybe you could spell it out for me," I snapped, irritated this twenty-year-old fashion statement had gotten the better of me.

She cocked her head and then laughed. "I don't think so."

Not knowing what else to do, I kept the gun trained on her and called Galloway. Voice mail.

"Argh!" I yelled, beyond frustrated. "Could you please pick up your phone? Sunny beach, but this can't wait. I'll call the station." I hung up, and while my attention was on my phone, Megan charged. We went down in a pile of limbs, but one thing Megan Sullivan hadn't anticipated was that I'm a scrappy fighter, and I don't fight fair. Granted, she didn't have gonads to crush my knee into, but a well-placed knee could still make a woman's eyes water, and I used it to great effect.

I still had the gun, and I was doing my utmost to not shoot her yet keep ahold of it because I had no doubt that she would not hesitate to shoot me should she get her hands on it. Grabbing a fistful of her hair, I pulled hard. She headbutted me, and I saw stars, but despite being dazed, I kept ahold of the gun, even when I felt her fingers wrap around it and try to pry it from my hand.

It discharged, the resulting bang loud, making my ears ring and bits of plaster rain down from the ceiling.

"Now, look what you've done!" I yelled.

She took advantage of my disorientation and jumped on my back. I swung around in a circle with her hanging off me, staggering to stay upright. She slung one arm around my throat and squeezed, cutting off my air supply. Leaning as far forward as I could manage, I suddenly flung my head backward, the back of my skull connecting with her face with a satisfying crunch. Her grip loosened, and I charged backward, slamming her into the wall.

She fell to the floor, blood pouring from her nose, and I promptly sat on her, and that's how Galloway found us minutes later.

"Oh, hey." I grinned then winced at the pressure on my bruised lip. I was having trouble seeing out of one eye and suspected I had the makings of a pretty good shiner.

Galloway stood in the doorway with his hands on his hips, surveying the scene. His eyes did a thorough inspection of my face, and I saw the flash of concern before he turned his attention to Megan.

"You can get off her now, Audrey." He whipped out his handcuffs and approached.

I was still holding the gun and gingerly held it out to him. "Take this, will you, before I accidentally shoot myself."

"You can give it to me if you like." Megan grunted. "I'd happily shoot you."

Ignoring her, Galloway took the gun, checked the safety was on, then tucked it into his belt. He held out a hand, and I placed mine in it, allowing him to help me to my feet. Our chests touched briefly, and I heard him draw in a deep breath. "You okay?" His words were low and deep, whispered in my ear.

"I'm fine," I said, overly loud. The gun going off may have damaged my hearing.

Galloway hauled Megan to her feet, spun her to face the wall, and cuffed her wrists behind her back while reading her Miranda rights. Straightening my clothes, I headed outside, passing Sergeant Addison Young and Officer Noah Walsh on the way.

"Woah, Audrey, you're looking a little rough," Addison said. "Do we need to call an ambulance for you?"

"Pft, no. These," I pointed to my face, "are just bruises."

"There's blood on your shirt," Noah pointed out.

"Not mine. But that reminds me." I pivoted and was about to head back inside when Galloway led Megan out. I stepped forward, forcing them to halt. "Don't throw rocks at animals!" I yelled so loudly she flinched. "It's mean. And it's animal cruelty." I shifted my attention to Galloway, who stood there with a sappy grin on his face. "Can you add that to the charges? What?" I frowned, confused. What was so funny?

"You're shouting," he said.

"It's because my ears are still ringing," I shouted in reply. "The gun went off. Oh, shoot. I'm not liable for damages, am I? Cos I'm not paying to have that ceiling repaired. It's her gun."

"No, you're not liable, relax." Galloway handed Megan off to Addison and Noah, who took her to the waiting patrol car. "I know you can't hear yourself properly, but trust me, the rest of us can."

I made an effort to lower my voice. "Okay. Better?"

"Better." He stepped forward and tilted my face up to the light, examining my bruises. A fat lip and a black eye weren't too bad in the whole scheme of things. "How do you feel?" he asked, thumb gently rubbing across my chin.

"Honestly, I'm fine. The adrenaline hasn't worn off yet. Speaking of bruises, how's Jay?"

"Awake. And happy to talk."

"And?"

"Dropped Megan right in it. She's behind it all."

"That's what's got me puzzled," I admitted. "I

swear I saw her buying drugs from Jay. How could that be if she's the dealer?"

"It was a setup. She knew you were there and needed to get you off her tail. What better way than to have you think she was buying recreational drugs? That she was the victim. More or less."

"And Jay went along with it?"

"Jay was clueless. She came up with some convoluted tale that they had a bad batch, and a buyer needed refunding and that she couldn't get back to the house—here—to deal with it, so she gave him the drugs, and he gave her the cash to give back to the so-called client."

"And he fell for that?"

Galloway shrugged. "Apparently."

Smart girl. It worked. She'd set me up, and I'd taken the bait.

"You think she killed Dean?"

Before he could answer, there was a shout from the garage, and Officer Tom Collier stuck his head out. "Galloway?" he called. "Found something."

I tagged along. Inside the garage was Megan's red hatch. I smacked my forehead. *Of course!* This was what Dean saw the night he died. A car coming down the street but turning off before my house. Because she'd driven into Mrs. Hill's empty garage.

"Whatcha got?" Galloway asked, snapping on his gloves.

Tom held up a blonde wig.

"It was her," I said out loud. She'd worn the wig to make herself look like Leah. To frame her should anyone see her car that night. I had to give it to her. She was certainly cunning. "Is that enough to prove she killed Dean, though?"

Galloway paused in inspecting the wig. "The wig alone? No. But the trace of blood not only on the wig but the glove box? If it's a match for Dean Ward, then yes, most definitely, she's going down for murder."

# 17

Ignoring the two ghosts standing on my driveway, I gave my statement then returned home.

"I can't believe it was Megan," Dean said, voice incredulous. "I've known her since she was a kid! She always seemed so sweet."

I snorted. "Sweet isn't the word I'd use. From the very few interactions I've had with her, snarky seems to cover it." Although that time at the hospital, when Amy had overdosed… I wondered now if Megan's concern had been an act. Had she intentionally dosed her friend to move suspicion away from herself?

"What happens now?" Dean asked, rubbing his

hands together. Ben and I looked at each other then around my living room. Usually, at this point, a white light would appear, but not in Dean's case. Nothing. Nothing happened, and I groaned. I wasn't sure I could cope with another full-time ghost. Ben, I could manage because he was my best friend, and being able to see and talk to him was worth it. But Dean? For starters, I didn't like him that much. I had no desire to have him hanging around twenty-four-seven.

"Keep your eye out for a very bright light. If you see it, walk into it," I instructed, heading into the bathroom to survey the damage to my face. A dark bruise was forming on my cheekbone, eye, and temple, and my bottom lip was fat and turning purple. But it hadn't split, and there was no blood. Grabbing a clean washcloth, I ran it under the faucet and pressed it to my bruised skin then returned to the living room where I flopped onto the sofa, keeping the washcloth pressed to my face.

"Is that it?" Dean wailed. "Keep an eye out? Some PI you are."

"Hey," Ben snapped. "She solved your murder."

"Accidentally," I said. I'd still been gunning for Leah when I'd stumbled onto Megan and her diabolical plan.

"How did Megan know I was on to her when I wasn't actually on to her?" Dean asked.

"Excellent question. I've no idea."

"Wait," Ben said, tapping his chin. "You said you decided to hire Audrey after finding that empty bag and the phone number on the napkin, right?"

"Well, yeah, kind of. I rang the number first, and when the person answered but didn't speak, that sort of confirmed for me that something was going on."

Ben and I looked at each other.

"It was Megan who answered the phone," Ben said.

I nodded, snapping my fingers. "I bet she recognized your voice, Dean. After all, you and her dad would have talked a lot over the years. She's heard you on the phone before."

"Right."

"That's when she ditched the phone," Ben said.

"Yeah, but why ditch it in her own bin? That's crazy." Dean rubbed a hand around the back of his neck, deep in thought.

"Not if you're trying to frame someone else. Think about it." I held up my hand to tick off on my fingers. "Eric's cufflinks found under your bed, yet he'd never set foot in your apartment. A blonde driving Megan's car—which we later discover is a wig. Of course, she'd dump the phone in her own bin. She wanted it to look like Leah had dumped the phone."

"She clearly knew about the affair between her dad and Leah." Ben crossed his arms and leaned back in the armchair he was currently hovering over.

"And decided she'd make Leah pay for it." Dean sighed, looking sad.

Just then, the hairs on the back of my neck tingled, and a feeling of doom slid over me. Through the wall, the three dark spirits appeared. I bolted upright, hand to my chest. Dean was right. They certainly seemed to be following him around.

Jumping to my feet, I held out my hand in a stop motion and demanded, "Who are you? What do you want? Don't you know it's rude to just walk through someone's wall?"

The spirits stopped and slowly turned my way, black mist rolling off them to creep across the floor. I swallowed, my brief moment of bravery rapidly disappearing. To my utter astonishment, the spirits began to take form. The black dissipated to reveal three middle-aged men dressed as 1920s gangsters, complete with tank tops and suspenders, bowler hats, and cigar stubs. All of them struck a resemblance to Al Capone.

"Hi, doll," one of them spoke, stepping forward while I took a corresponding step back, only to bump into the sofa and fall on my butt on the cushions. "She can see us, boys!"

"So, what's your beef?" Another stepped forward, cracking his knuckles, which would have been more effective if you could actually hear the cracking of said knuckles.

"Beef?" I gulped.

"Yeah, you know, problem? Yeah, what's your problem, doll?"

The first man took off his hat and slapped his companion with it. "She already told you, you sap. She don't like you walking through her walls, see? It's im-po-lite." He turned to me and offered a bow. "Allow me to introduce myself. I'm Tommy. This here is Bruno." He indicated the knuckle-cracking ghost. "And he's Arnold." He jerked a thumb at the third ghost. They all looked so similar with their slicked-back hair and smoothly-shaven faces.

"Right." I nodded.

"And you are?"

"Audrey Fitzgerald, Private Investigator." I

pushed to my feet, feeling at a distinct disadvantage having Tommy tower over me.

"She's a dick?" Arnold hooted.

"Well, that's just swell." Tommy cocked his hat, giving him a rakish look. "At least you're not the fuzz; you're just a gumshoe."

I had no idea what he was saying. If I'd known they were coming, I'd have brushed up on my 1920s slang.

Ben finally spoke up. "I think they're saying that at least you're not with the police. What can we do for you, gentlemen?"

Bruno eyed him up and down, bumping his fist into the open palm of his other hand in a definite threat.

Tommy jerked his head, and Bruno grumbled beneath his breath but stopped the threatening behavior.

"You're a good-looking broad," Tommy said. "But we don't want no trouble, see."

"Neither do I," I assured him. "Are you looking for help to cross over?"

All three men looked at me, then each other, and burst out laughing.

"What a gal," Arnold chortled with great mirth.

"Why would we want that? After we popped the big one, we were free. Why change that?"

I shrugged. Partly because I wasn't one hundred percent sure what he'd said, but I figured it was along the lines of their deaths gave them great freedom, and they didn't see any point in crossing over or moving on. That was my interpretation anyway.

"Once we saw them take away the skirt in bracelets, we figured we'd find our grifter here."

"You're here for Dean?" Ben asked, indicating the pale-faced ghost currently standing behind Ben as if he could protect him.

"Fellow bootlegger. Figure it's time we brought in some new blood."

Dean blinked. "You want me to join your… gang?"

"He's finally using his noodle," Bruno grunted, while Tommy nodded, half his mouth curling in a grin. "Whaddaya say? Ready to blow this joint?"

Before Dean could answer, Tommy turned his attention to me. "Apologies, doll, for walking through ya wall. We'll be leaving ya in peace. You coming?" As quickly as his attention had been on me, it turned to Dean.

"Well?" I prompted. "You going?" *Please say yes, please say yes.*

"It depends. Where are we going?"

"Chicago!" Tommy declared, rubbing his hands together. "There's a grifter there I've had me eye on, great-grandson of a doll I used to know. Ah, Daisy, but she was a bearcat."

"Chicago?" Dean repeated. "Sounds good. Count me in."

Ben and I watched with our mouths hanging open as the four ghosts evaporated into a dark mist and disappeared through the wall.

"Well. That was..." Ben began.

"Unexpected?" I filled in for him. I'd thought the spirits were malicious, but it turned out they were relatively harmless gangsters. Although I doubted they'd appreciate being thought of as harmless.

"What's next?" Ben asked.

"Dinner at my folks' house."

---

"We're going to need a bigger dining room," Dad joked, watching his grandchildren, Isabelle, Madeline, and Nathaniel, as they sat on a picnic rug in the adjacent living room, shoving mac 'n cheese into their mouths. Grace was asleep in her stroller, and I joined Laura and Mom, who were peering in at her, totally smitten. And who could blame them? She was adorable.

"I can't believe you're out of the hospital already," I said to Laura. To be honest, I couldn't believe she was upright and walking around. There had been so much blood. And pain. A shudder rippled through me.

"They don't keep you in long these days, especially if it's not your first," Laura explained. "How are you doing?"

"I'm fine." I smiled then winced at the pressure on my lip.

"I don't mean your face. That'll heal. I mean, how are you holding up after witnessing the birth of your niece?"

"Other than the PTSD? I'm fine," I teased. And I was. Sort of. I still wasn't sure I wanted kids, but Galloway made a valid point. I didn't need to decide right now. There was time.

"Audrey? Please, come sit," Amanda called, and I turned to see her standing next to a chair in the dining room, a cold pack in her hand. "Let me put this on that eye. It'll help with the swelling."

"Okaaaay." I looked from Laura to Amanda and

back again. "This is weird, right? She's being weird?" I said under my breath.

"She's definitely being weird," Laura agreed. "Normally, she'd be chastising you for using your face to block Megan's punches. But not a peep out of her."

"It's the bet. I won the bet." I nodded.

"Good to see she's keeping up her end of the bargain." Although Laura's eyes had narrowed as we both eyeballed our sister-in-law.

"Let's see how long it lasts, huh?" I grinned then did Amanda's bidding, making myself comfortable on the dining chair while she handed me the cold pack. It did, indeed, feel divine against my aching cheekbone and eye socket. Maybe, just maybe, Amanda and I had turned a corner in our relationship, and she'd finally quit trying to fix me. I guess time would tell.

"I have something else for you," Amanda said, disappearing into the kitchen only to return moments later, carrying a tray laden with a selection of food.

She set it down in front of me, and the aroma of coffee wafted in the air. I leaned forward and inhaled, my aching face forgotten.

"Amanda's been baking all afternoon," Mom said

proudly. "Go ahead, Amanda, tell Audrey what they are."

Amanda pointed. "Here you have café mocha cookies, espresso chocolate chunk brownies, coffee cake muffins, coffee roasted sweet potato fries, and finally, coffee rubbed steak."

I blinked. "Wow. You've outdone yourself."

"You won the bet fair and square." She chewed her lip, unable to resist a final parting shot. "Just… limit the consumption of these. Please? You'll be bouncing off the walls if you eat all that at once, and honestly, I don't think your face can take anymore."

"Relax, Amanda. I wouldn't dream of it. Here. Have a café mocha cookie." I held out the plate of cookies, and Amanda took one, nibbling at it with her even white teeth. I turned my attention back to the tray laden with coffee-flavored food. Finally, after dreaming of such delights all week, my dreams had turned into reality.

"Come on, everyone, help me out here. Amanda is actually right. If I eat all of this myself, I'll be tweaking until next week. Dig in."

"Wait," Dustin said. "Did I hear you correctly? Did you just say Amanda was right?"

"Har har." I threw a brownie at him, and it

bounced off his head. Galloway caught it before it hit the floor.

"Good catch." I laughed.

He winked at me and took a bite of the brownie. "I know."

---

Check out book six, ***Who Ghost There?***: https://janehinchey.com/WhoGhostThere

# AFTERWORD

Thank you for reading, if you enjoyed **Here Ghost Nothing**, please consider leaving a review.

If you'd like to find a complete list of my books, including series and reading order, please visit my website at:

**https://janehinchey.com**

Also, if you'd like to sign up to receive emails with the latest news, exclusive offers and more, you can do that here:

**Janehinchey.com/join-my-newsletter**

And finally, if social media is your jam, you're

welcome to join my readers group, Jane's Little Devils, on Facebook here:

**https://www.facebook.com/groups/JanesLittleDevils/**

Thank you so much for taking a chance and reading my book - I do this for you.

xoxo

Jane

## READ MORE BY JANE

**Find them all RIGHT HERE**

**The Ghost Detective Paranormal Cozy Mystery Series**

#1 Ghost Mortem

#2 Give up the Ghost

#3 The Ghost is Clear

#4 A Ghost of a Chance

#5 Here Ghost Nothing

---

**Witch Way Paranormal Cozy Mystery Series**

#1 Witch Way to Magic & Mayhem

#2 Witch Way to Romance & Ruin

#3 Witch Way Down Under

#4 Witch Way to Beauty & the Beach

#5 Witch Way to Death & Destruction

#6 Witch Way to Secrets & Sorcery

---

## Paranormal Romance

**The Awakening Series**

#1 First Blade

#2 First Witch

#3 First Blood

# ABOUT JANE

**Find all my stories RIGHT HERE!**

Hi there! I'm Jane Hinchey, bestselling author of the Ghost Detective Cozy Mystery Series. I totally admit that I can be a snarky, sarcastic, and on the odd occasion, *hilarious* storyteller. I love writing anything paranormal, from murder mysteries to steamy romance, but I've discovered everything I write has an element of suspense in it. Just like life, right? You never know how your story is going to end up!

I'm an Aussie – British born, Australian raised, which makes for an interesting vocabulary on occasion, especially as I write using US English. Let's not get started on hood versus bonnet, torch versus flashlight, thong versus flip flop… believe me, that last one can get a girl into *a lot* of trouble if used incorrectly.

My life is pretty simple. I love reading, cats, and my family. My hero is my dad. I'm short in height but big on imagination. While I can't technically speak feline, I often have animated conversations with my ginger ninja, Maxx, and my derpy cat, Morgan.

I live by three simple rules – (1) smile every day. (2) Be kind to each other. (3) Follow your dreams. And bonus rule, always, *always,* have coffee on hand!

I ABSOLUTELY love talking to readers (especially when they send me photos of their pets!) Send me a message ANYTIME at www.JaneHinchey.com or on Facebook at https://www.facebook.com/JaneHincheyAuthor

XOXO
Jane

CPSIA information can be obtained
at www.ICGtesting.com
Printed in the USA
BVHW082212051221
623306BV00005B/108